Gladness in My Heart

GLADNESS IN MY HEART

by
GRACE WATKINS
Author of *That Certain Radiance*

ZONDERVAN PUBLISHING HOUSE
Grand Rapids, Michigan

To
BILL
"Thou hast put gladness in my heart."
Psalm 4:7

Gladness in My Heart

CHAPTER ONE

Writing with the left hand is more difficult than I first thought. As with a child's first grasping of a pencil, my scrawl refuses to behave as my mind dictates. But there is nothing else to do. I cannot walk, or play the piano, or knit. I can read, but after weeks of unrelieved reading, even books become tiresome.

Outside, it is beginning to snow. I cannot feel it, but a raw wind nips at the branches of the elm trees, now barren of all covering. The flower bulbs have long since gone to sleep. The lawn, a velvety emerald from April to October, has turned a dull olive. Soon it will be white. A gray squirrel, tardy in his nut-gathering, is frantically dashing from bottom to top of the giant oak tree directly across the drive. I would like to be out there with him. I would like to be anywhere, but in this cast.

Strange that even simple abilities like stretching for a yawn, or reaching for a dropped pencil, when denied, assume the proportions of a magnificent blessing. I think now, *If I could walk across the room, I would never again complain.* But would I? Probably.

I have no one to blame but myself. If I hadn't been so foolish — but occasionally the Lord uses a foolish act — or would He find some other way, less painful, less searing in its scar, if we would stand back and let Him work?

Nothing in the last eighteen months seemed to lead up to this — not a hint of foreboding, no dogs howling eerily in the night to warn of pending doom. Maybe that sort of thing only happens in books. And this isn't really a book — it's the story of the beginning of our life together. . . .

Marriage doesn't begin with a wedding — or even with a honeymoon. These serve only as a prelude. Marriage begins with the first real housekeeping — whether in an attic apartment or a

9

mortgaged ranch home. Like that of most of our friends, ours began most humbly.

It wasn't much of an apartment. The end one in a dingy yellow barracks-type building, it was no better nor worse than the rest of the housing thrown up as "temporary" quarters for married students. Row on ugly row these barracks stood, and no one remembered they had not been intended for permanence. At the base of the Appalachian foothills, where beauty ran wild, the scar of human structure remained, an insult to the Creator.

But the sun cast long shadowy fingers across the jewelled green of this afternoon late in June. At the end of the bulldozed clearing, a triple row of tall junipers and spruce met a tumbling mountain stream, whose perpetual bubble provided background music for nine months of the year.

We drew up and parked the car, getting out slowly, taking in all our surroundings with new eyes. After struggling with an ill-fitting key in a creaky lock, Bruce flung open the door, then in a chivalrous gesture, he carried me over the threshhold.

"Welcome home, Mrs. King," he began. The effect of gallantry was somewhat marred when his heel caught on the doorsill, and he staggered into the kitchen, dumping me unceremoniously on the plain wooden table apparently placed there for the purpose. The smell of new paint, insufficiently aired, nearly asphyxiated us.

"Could we open a window?" I gasped.

Late afternoon coolness rushed in to relieve our parched noses. Hand in hand, we surveyed our domain, no less endowed than Adam and Eve in the first garden. Possessing neither beauty nor luxury, it was adequate for our needs. A battered gas stove, an old refrigerator, a chipped wooden table with four straight chairs completed the furnishings in the kitchen. Off this room, opened three doors — one to the outside, the next to a minuscule bathroom (it was several years before we boasted a bathtub of our own) and the last to our bedroom. Crowded with a double bed, a tall dresser and a sturdy old desk of the roll top variety, there was barely room for two of us to dress at the same time.

In a flow of possessive tenderness I gushed, "Oh, Bruce, I'm a housewife!"

He arched a mocking eyebrow. "I never heard the role described so enthusiastically. Do you think you'll like it? Keeping house for me?"

"I'll love it!" I promised. "Let's bring in our wedding presents. Did I remember to tell you I can't cook?"

10

Unconcerned, he shrugged. "That's okay. The Army issued iron linings for stomachs in Korea. What do you want in first?"

"I never really had time to learn," I apologized. "Every summer I worked, and this summer I was going to learn, but then you didn't want to wait till August, so——"

"So you can read. That's what cook books are for, I understand." His crooked grin spread across his craggy features, lighting up his deep blue eyes, and I was convinced a handsomer man had never breathed.

We had been married for twenty-six hours, and our rapture enveloped the entire world. We walked in a golden glow of well-being, forming our own mutual admiration society.

"You're wonderful."

"I know. And humble, too."

"And smart."

"Very. I married you."

"And handsome."

He stroked his unshaven chin. "Uh-huh. Do you like my beard that much?"

"I might if you could get it past the porcupine stage."

"Tomorrow I'll sneak out of bed at five so I can be nicely shaved when you wake up."

"And at the same time I'll sneak out of bed and comb my hair so I can be pretty when you wake me up."

He gathered me into his arms with a chuckle of exuberant delight. "Oh, Sandy, Sandy, how did I ever find you?"

We were so much in love it hurt.

For us, who thought we knew all about it, marriage held many surprises. Pulled apart for dissection by the analysts, explored in magazine articles by the experts, marriage is still not adequately described. "For better, for worse," proved superbly accurate wording.

Minor irritations arose. He did not like it when I left the top off the toothpaste tube. I resented his intrusion of my privacy — his keys and coins on my otherwise tidy dresser — his coat across the back of a chair. But the most common source of friction among newly-weds — money — posed no problem for us. There simply wasn't any. We had not a cent for a cup of coffee or an extra ball point pen. From Bruce's allotment, we paid our tithe, our rent, and our electric bill. Our car stood idle in the drive for want of gasoline in its tank. We ate for less than ten dollars a week. A jar of vaseline and a bottle of aspirin cured all the ills we could afford.

But the horn of plenty overflowed for us — with laughter, with joy, with unsuspected depths of love — with all the thrill of exploring another's being, and finding it just short of perfect.

We learned to know each other in a way undreamed of in our courting days. It was a wonderful summer, a rainbow-hued summer, with promise of eternal bliss in a garden of joy.

Housecleaning in those tiny quarters took precious little time. While Bruce sweltered in summer school sessions, I sat under an overhanging white pine, with my bare feet in the icy mountain brook which ran downstream just a few hundred yards from our door. And I read and read and read. All the books I had been missing for the last four years — devotions, bestsellers, plays and classics. Occasionally, my conscience would smite me, for it seemed incredible that there really wasn't anything to do!

I could have found a job to augment our income. But we'd been through a virtual battle over that. I had been ill the previous winter; though I was fully recovered now, Bruce still bore in mind a fragile wisp of a girl. He wanted me to wait till fall to begin teaching. So I luxuriated in wonderful free time that summer, the only period in my life when I could do exactly as I wished.

The marigolds and zinnias outside our kitchen door bloomed in a blend of bright yellows, pinks, and purples. They were my children — I expected everyone to admire them.

We visited with the neighbors, all as impoverished as we were. The wives exchanged recipes for tuna fish and hamburger casseroles, laughed at the idiosyncrasies of men, wondered at the miracle of children. They were good friends, but friends only for the season. Now I can barely recall their names.

Bruce was not much of a man about the house. He rarely wiped dishes and never carried out the garbage. I wonder what he thought happened to it? But in other ways he tried to be helpful.

One afternoon I came in from watering my flower patch, to discover my husband of two weeks standing in the middle of the kitchen floor, with half an inch of soapy water all about him. His feet were bare, and his pants rolled up to his knees.

"What happened?" I gasped.

"I'm going to scrub the floor," he announced expansively. "I need the exercise, and it's too big a job for you."

Unaccustomed to being treated like a delicate lily, I leaned against the doorjamb. "But why did you slosh it all over the floor?"

He looked a little doubtful. "This is the way they do it in the Navy."

"The Navy has ocean all around to take up the excess. How are you going to do it?"

"Don't we have a sponge?"

"No. And we don't have very many rags. Besides, you weren't in the Navy. You were in the Army."

"We traveled to Korea by ship." He paused long enough to scratch his head. "You know, I never thought of taking it up. I just figured the floor would soak clean quicker this way."

It was a shame to discourage his burst of helpfulness by laughing. But mirth could no more be contained than children after the schoolbell has rung. We mopped and wrung and giggled and mopped and wrung until every crack in the wooden floor was thoroughly swollen. Never since has it been so clean.

In those two months, Bruce changed a great deal. Gone were the moods of withdrawn aloofness. He learned to communicate — not idle small talk, for he never was good at that, but his aspirations, his deep thoughts, his plans for the future. He loved the Lord wholeheartedly. He put me to shame in his earnest prayers for guidance, and his belief that they would always be answered. He worked to achieve what comes naturally to the new-born infant — a child-like trust in the Lord's will.

On one subject, he was absolutely silent — his family. Yet he must have thought about them a great deal. He and his brother had been close. But for all we heard from them, they might have been non-existent. Never a postcard or telephone call to break the silence. Orphaned at the age of three, when both his parents had been killed in a collision, Bruce and his brother, Don, had been raised by their Uncle Larry, sent to the best boarding schools and summer camps, and given every privilege of the well-to-do, except the privilege of knowing a personal God. When Bruce, wounded in Korea, did find the Saviour, his uncle tried to ignore his new "fanaticism," hoping it would eventually wear off. It did not. It grew. Later, after we were engaged, Bruce and I made public our intention to become missionaries in a foreign land. It had been an ugly, nasty scene. Months passed before either of us eliminated the memory of Mr. King's white, contorted face, twisted with anguished fury, as he literally screamed,

"Get out! I don't want to see you again! Go back to that fanatical school and learn to be a thorough madman!"

Bruce's hurt had been so deep, that even now he could not talk about it. It was as if, by deliberately pushing it out of his memory, he could become another Bruce King.

And, in a sense, he had. He had set himself an impossible task, in trying to answer the Lord's call, and still keep his uncle happy. It had been a circus performance, straddling the backs of two horses headed in opposite directions. When he finally settled on the horse he would sit, his ride became more comfortable.

At first, we hoped the break was not irreconcilable. His brother, Don, served as best man at our wedding. Pat, Don's beautiful wife, took in my family happiness with tears in her eyes. In all her life, she had never encountered so much genuine family love.

"It's like a Currier and Ives painting," she breathed in her husky voice.

And Don, though wary at first, gradually allowed himself to be drawn into the warmth of our circle. They had only come to Bartlett the day before the wedding, when all was confusion, with cousins and aunts and uncles and deliverymen running in and out in constant activity. No one fussed over them, for everyone assumed they were there to help. Accustomed to hired caterers, servants and professional musicians, Don and Pat found the small-town wedding of a small-town girl a novel experience. They adjusted admirably, with Don exchanging wisecracks with my younger brother, and Pat cleaning celery in the kitchen with my sister. When, after the evening meal, our family gathered in the living room for devotions, they listened respectfully. We thought — we hoped — the rift would not extend to them. Neither of us had opportunity to feel them out on the subject during those hectic two days. And we did not hear from them afterwards. They were no longer under Uncle Larry's roof, for they had moved into their own home in June. Therefore we could only assume they intended to go their way and let us go ours. It was a silent grief for both of us, but much more for Bruce than for me. After all, I still had the Marshall family.

Bruce's summer school session was nearly over when a letter arrived from my father. In it was a check for twenty-five dollars "to cover your gas money home." They were planning a family camping trip to the White Mountains of New Hampshire, and they wanted us to go with them. I held my breath, waiting for Bruce's reaction. He possessed a touchy sort of pride which often forbade the open generosity of my parents. A shadow crossed his face momentarily as he glanced at the check.

"We don't have to go if you don't want to, Bruce," I said.

He turned the letter over in his hand, not quite looking at me. "Don't you like camping?"

"I love it. I haven't been for four years."

"I've never been. Let's go."

The easy victory shocked me. "Do you really want to?"

"Sure. I *hate* accepting money from your folks, but I love being with them. It seems I have to give up one or the other." He grinned a slow grin, revealing the considerable effort this pride-swallowing cost. I left my place at the table to plant a kiss on his forehead.

"Bruce, I think you're the nicest person in the world."

Though my husband had been reared in a "privileged" home, his opportunities at simple enjoyment had been "underprivileged." He had never caught a herring in his bare hands, or scrambled up a mountain in the early morning mist, or gathered blueberries for his own breakfast. But like a game, Bruce entered into the spirit of Marshall family camping with great zest. He helped unload the trailer in our shaded camping site along the Kancamagus Highway. But then, he could not tolerate the sight of my mother carrying a bucket of water from the pump a hundred yards up the road. He dropped the tent stake he was holding for Dad, to go help her with the pail, thus leaving my father somewhat exasperated.

"Never mind, Dad," I reminded him, as I stepped over to take Bruce's place, "at least you don't have to worry about how he treats me!"

"I never did," said my father. "You've always seemed more than adequately prepared to take care of yourself."

Bruce treated my father with great deference and respect, seeking his advice on everything from comprehensive Bible courses to the weight of oil to be used in the car. But for my mother was reserved all the love he would have showered on his own, had she lived. He enshrined motherhood in an idealistic aura rather out of keeping with the realistic world in which we lived. I would catch his gaze on her while she performed such menial tasks as scrubbing potatoes in the makeshift kitchen under our old black tarp.

Unashamedly, he explained, "I love to watch a woman in the kitchen. It seems the center of the universe."

"Or at least the hub of the family," I agreed, remembering

the many quiet hours of conversation we had spent around our kitchen table at home, where we learned as well as helped.

He was a big man, my husband, but a tender, sensitive one, not at all bothered by the need to prove his masculinity with roughness. Through his eyes, I saw my family in a new, appreciative light. My father, balding on top, with a scholarly stoop to his thin shoulders, and an understanding smile in his dark brown eyes — my mother, gently efficient, a halo of light behind her fading blonde hair — shy, reticent Carol, to whom music was the only avenue of freedom — and boisterous Ronnie, just emerging from the self-absorption of early adolescence. Ray, fifteen months older than I, was missing. But he was married and attending seminary in Texas. He could get home only once a year, and that at Christmas.

For New Hampshire, the weather behaved remarkably well. In the week and a half that we camped, we had only two sudden squalls. One caught us as we were halfway up Mount Cannon. I had desperately wanted Bruce to see Lonesome Lake in the bright sunlight with the fringe of perfect evergreens casting a double image in the deep blue mirror of the lake. Instead, dashing up the last quarter of the trail, we were forced to take refuge in the Ranger's shelter while the rain drummed a relentless hail across the slate colored water. We were soaking wet and shivering. When the young ranger in charge offered us a glass of Kool-Aid, we laughed in his face. He could not keep his eyes off Carol, who smiled in ethereal sweetness and answered in monosyllables.

Fifteen minutes later, to the ranger's disappointment and Carol's relief, the sun lined the clouds with a showy border of silver-gold. It spread across the lake — no longer a calm sapphire, but a turbulent blue-brown-green. We sat on the wooden dock to dry out. Gradually, the wind died, the sun pretended it had been shining all along, and the lake composed itself into the picture I had wanted Bruce to view.

In the evenings we sat about the campfire, telling stories, taking turns at Bible reading, catching our light from the sporadic flicker of the fire. Round the family circle we prayed, drawing closer to each other as we drew near the Heavenly Father.

Is the good life dull? The idea springs only from a sour grapes position. Ours was a good life. It wasn't dull.

CHAPTER TWO

In September, the mountains of upper New York leave the finest landscape artist at a loss. The very extravagance of color, attempted on canvas, would appear exaggerated. An early frost that year brought out the reds and yellows and burnt umbers in such a kaleidoscope of brilliance that our brains could scarcely capture what our eyes beheld. Each hilltop vied for honors in splendor of hue. We walked through an arch of pure gold as Harbrook's abundant maples whispered in wonder at their own display. For over two months it lasted, before winter's shrouding snows enveloped us in dignified quiet.

Now, at last, we began to settle into married life. All summer, like children in a dollhouse, we had played at the game. With our return for the fall semester, a tight schedule gripped us. Bruce, in his final months of study, had labs almost every afternoon, then studied far into the night. A meticulous, thorough worker, he amazed us both with a record of straight A's. Our courtship had been troubled; during this time he had not distinguished himself with scholastic achievement.

"See? You should have married me long ago," he teased, "and maybe I'd have graduated *cum laude.*"

"Actually, I should have married you before we met, and you could have graduated *summa cum laude,*" I agreed.

I became a schoolteacher. Five short words. Unsuspecting, perhaps blissfully unsuspecting, I had no previous conception of the challenge, the discouragement, the sheer bone weariness which make up a schoolteacher's life. I entered my chosen career with a certain cockiness. I liked young people, had a sense of humor, and had studied all the prescribed child psychology courses. In addition, my father was a high school principal, and I had been

17

exposed to the "problem child's problems" all my life. Frankly, I considered myself very well prepared.

Harbrook Academy students were divided roughly into three groups; missionary's youngsters who had been left at home for their high school years; town kids, who posed comparatively few problems; and problem children whose parents had lost control of them at home. This last segment had been sent to Harbrook Academy in hopes that a Christian faculty would cure their ills. In some cases, where the difficulties were of short standing, it did. In other cases, sending trouble-makers away from home only increased their inner turmoil. It showed.

They were individuals in their own right. No development charts traced their courses accurately. What worked for one failed miserably for another. The goad of competition sparked some; discouraged others. I made all the mistakes in the book, and invented a few of my own. I was over-strict when I should have been sympathetic, lenient when I should have been firm. From day to day my disciplinary tactics wavered uncertainly, and it took no time at all for my seventh graders to have me pegged. After all, there were 83 of them to study only four teachers; in reverse, we four had 83 to study. The kids had the advantage and kept it.

Night after night, I fell into bed, too exhausted to think. I could not quit, for there was no one to take my place. Nor would I have considered it, except in some idle dreaming in which I harked back to the good old pre-teaching days. I wanted to succeed as a teacher — I felt that, deep inside me, were the makings of a fairly good one — but I could not dredge up the best because I was too busy with non-essentials.

English Seven-One I came to dread as a mighty tug-o-war between learning and antics. Trouble always boasts its ring leader. Her name was Miriam McCartney. She pulled her red-gold hair back into a tight pony-tail, which she switched constantly. Light, almost invisible eyebrows and lashes fringed her pale blue eyes. A mouth, too large for genuine beauty, curved in a provocative smile. Miriam was precocious in every way except mental. Neither liked by her peers, nor accepted by older girls, she turned to the one sure source of attention. It was not difficult to imagine her on the back seat of some boy's car on a lonely, unlighted road.

She had a knack of keeping one ear turned to class instruction, while causing subtle disturbance in the back of the room, where she was surrounded by boys a head shorter than she. When I tried to catch her with sudden questions, she always had an answer, not necessarily the right one. No matter what her reply,

18

it always evoked loud guffaws from that corner. I could have forced her to sit in the front row. Somehow, I sensed this would serve only to antagonize, not tame her. Miriam virtually dared a superior to discipline her so she could prove she didn't care.

One Monday morning, the boil churned to a head. Papers were being passed back and forth within the "inner circle," accompanied by surreptitious snickers. It took little imagination to guess at their content. In cowardice, I wanted to ignore them, for I was uncertain what to do. Even that became an impossible tactic. So little was their respect for me, that the culprits hardly bothered to conceal their movements. In mid-sentence, I stepped quickly to the back of the room and confiscated the drawings. Expectant silence fell across the room. My sickened eyes absorbed the etchings one by one.

One cannot go through public school without encountering the usual terms of cheap filth. Perhaps the human mind reverts to this naturally. Miriam's sketches carried an air of sinister perversion. What could a thirteen-year-old girl understand of this?

There were four of them. I stacked them neatly, then ripped them lengthwise. In an instant, she was on her feet, her pale eyes flashing in desperation. Four inches taller and fifteen pounds heavier, she towered above me.

"Give them to me! They're mine! You can't have them, you——!"

I wanted to slap her. Hard, across the face. Wipe that insolent sneer right off her mouth. Only God knows what restrained me. I did push her, roughly, back into her seat.

"Sit down! And stay there!" I barked. Then, with great deliberation, I shredded her prized drawings into confetti.

"Don't move until I give you permission," I growled through my teeth.

Meekly, the boys swung around in their places, hands folded sedately on their desks. As one, the class let out a breath of relief. The moment had passed. But not for a moment would I ignore Miriam.

I kept my eyes on her all through the dull discussion of adverbial clauses. I hadn't realized it was possible to keep a clear mind on such divergent subjects. It was like having two compartments of the brain, both functioning separately and well.

Miriam's pale face had grown sheet white. At first, she sat rigid, furious in her restraint. Gradually, her muscles relaxed and she began to fidget. I paused for just a second with raised eyebrows, and she tensed again. The class bell rang. Miriam rose to leave with her division, but I halted her.

"Miriam, you have not been given permission to move," I reminded her in a toneless voice. She sat back.

Whatever explanation was offered to her other teachers, I do not know. I received no inquiries as to her absence. Through two periods she sat, wilted but defiant. The incoming divisions wondered at her presence, but knew enough not to ask aloud.

The one free period of my day arrived — time I ordinarily used to review the history subject I would teach after lunch.

"Miriam, come up here where we can talk," I suggested calmly.

In a teary voice, she replied, "May I please go to the ladies' room?"

I was not about to relent. I had watched these wild girls operate in high school. They would employ any emotion common to the female gender to twist a teacher about their fingers — particularly feigned remorse.

"Go and come back. Do not speak to anyone on the way."

She returned, her blue eyes red-rimmed. She took the first seat in the row directly in front of the teacher's desk. A stir of pity moved in my heart. She was only a little girl in a woman's body.

"Now, Miriam, tell me about these drawings. Were they originals?"

"What do you mean?"

"I mean, did you copy them from someone else, or did you think them up yourself?"

"I copied them."

Outside our window, two bluejays squawked in a flurry of circular flight, quarreling over a crumb of bread. The sunlight lay in great patches of cheer across the green lawn. It was much too clean a day for this filth. With great reluctance, I turned back.

"Do you understand them?"

She shrugged her shoulders. "Sure. Are you going to expel me?"

"What would happen to you if you were expelled?"

Her lips stretched in an unconvincing grin. "The old man would find another school."

"How many have you been in?"

"This is the third. I stayed back two years."

"You're fifteen, then?"

20

"Yeah."

"Did you leave the other schools because you were asked to?"

"Not asked. They kicked me out." She took perverse pride in this fact, certain that getting the best of adults was life's supreme delight.

"For the same reason?"

"I don't remember."

"Your parents — if I called them for a conference, would they be able to come?"

"I dunno. They'd have to, if I was being kicked out."

"Do you want to be expelled?"

"I don't care. One stupid place is no different from another stupid place."

"Do you care about anything?"

"I dunno. Just give me a pencil and paper — drawing's all I care about."

"You could become a fine artist, Miriam. Your lines are sure and deft. There are better sources of material, though."

"Draw what brings the money, my old man says. He's a commercial artist."

Was that where Miriam's ideas were born? I dared not ask.

"And your mother?"

"*Which* mother? I've had three." Her tone was hardened and cynical as an old crone's. "That's why the old man shipped me off to school — to get rid of me. His latest wife didn't want me in the house."

"What happened to your real mother? Why aren't you with her?"

"She couldn't stand me, either." Again Miriam lapsed into sullen discomfort. Her pale eyes gazed past me, out of the window. Only the slightest quiver of her chin betrayed any feeling. I could have wept. Restless under the quiet, she turned back.

"Are you going to expel me?"

"No. I can't expel you. I'm only a teacher. Such a drastic measure would have to be enacted by the principal and faculty. And I've destroyed the evidence. Is there any more?"

"In my room. You want to see them?"

"I want you to burn them. *All* of them. And produce no more."

She stood up, a sardonic grin across her features! "Is that all?"

"Not quite. Tuesday and Thursday afternoons I want you

21

to come to my house immediately after school and stay till supper. I think your sick mind needs attention."

"Oh, I see," she sneered. "Sort of a Big Sister affair, huh?"

"No!" I snapped. "I'm not your Big Sister. And I'm not your friend, or your counselor. I'm your jailer!"

In stocking feet, I stood five feet three. Of slender build, I had never reached one hundred and ten pounds. But if toughness were all Miriam McCartney respected, toughness she would get.

"Okay," she said, a new light in her eyes. "I'll report — to *jail* — tomorrow afternoon."

I stood in the doorway, watching, as she swung jauntily down the hall, her sweater slung carelessly over one shoulder. She could have been a barefoot youngster on her way to the fishing stream.

"Any trouble, Mrs. King?" came a quiet voice from behind. The high school principal had approached so silently she startled me.

"Some," I admitted. "I'll tell you about it later. Now I want to see what happens."

"She's a hard one," agreed Mrs. Stibbe. "You're not alone with these youngsters. We'll all help when we can."

With her streaked gray hair pulled into a tight bun at the back of her neck, Mrs. Stibbe looked as severe as an early Pilgrim. Devoid of all makeup, her face was seamed with deep wrinkles. Even to black cotton stockings, her clothes were invariably dark and unshapely. To personal comeliness she paid not the slightest heed. But when she smiled, her dark hazel eyes lit up with kindliness and good humor. Her soft voice lilted in gentle cadences. She was an old-fashioned saint.

Bruce listened gravely as I described the day's events. He was not shocked, as I had been, but he had not seen the sketches. He protested, "Sandy, you're not a trained psychologist. You shouldn't have told her to come here. She'll wear you ragged, and you're too tired to think straight, as it is."

"Someone has to extend a helping hand!" I cried.

"Do you think no one else has tried?"

"We can't give up on her! She's only fifteen!"

"You're only twenty-two! It isn't enough age difference for her to respect you, or for you to know how to cope with her twisted mentality."

"Please, Bruce," I pled. "I need you to back me up, not undermine me."

He took me in his arms to kiss my forehead at the hairline.

22

"It isn't the goodness of your heart I question, dear. Just your good sense. Keep detached from this girl or she'll weigh you down."

I tried. Miriam was at my door Tuesday afternoon a bare five minutes after I had arrived. She slouched in the kitchen chair I offered her, too worldly-weary to sit up straight.

English Seven-One had proceeded without a hitch that morning. Miriam's cohorts who had done all the snickering the day before now detached themselves from all acquaintance with the girl. They weren't bad kids, any of them. Boylike, they naturally regarded any teacher as "the Enemy," but Miriam's flagrant violation of classroom etiquette had been too much for them. For a change, I had twenty-one little paragons of virtue in class. We covered twice the material discussed on previous days.

I looked at Miriam closely. Her face was peaked, her eyes unhappy. She leafed through the Bible lying on the kitchen table.

"I know why you asked me down here," she began by way of prelude. "You want to talk to me about my soul."

The girl was clever. By keeping one step ahead of her antagonist, she could force him into a defensive position.

"Why do you say that?"

"Because that's what all you salvationists do. You're concerned for my soul. What happens in Heaven — does God keep a little black book with check marks for each Christian? One for you, and one for him, and one for her——"

She was enjoying her own singsong.

"You're suspicious of everyone, Miriam. Why? Hasn't anyone ever been good to you?"

"Not that I can recall. The world's a rotten place to live! D'you think they'd send me to the moon if I asked?"

I cut us each a piece of lemon cake and poured her a glass of milk. She picked up her fork and proceeded to eat. Misery had not conquered her appetite.

"You could travel to the farthest galaxy, Miriam. But you'll still carry the rottenness with you. You need to be changed from the inside out."

"Then change me!" With the fluid motion of a tawny jungle cat, she stood up and stretched.

I shook my head. "I can't."

"Yeah, I know. Only God can do that. My roommate told me. She said it was her duty to witness to me." Miriam picked up her fork again and took another bite.

"Do you like your roommate?"

"She doesn't like me."

"Why?"

"I dunno. Why don't you like me? Why doesn't anyone like me?"

"You don't let us. Every gesture of friendship is slapped back in our faces. You think there's an angle to everything. You're so full of hate and unhappiness that you would prefer to change everyone over to what you are, than to change yourself."

"You mean about those pictures?" She brought up the subject. I would not have.

"You deliberately set out to corrupt those young boys, Miriam. You *know* they are years younger than you in worldly experience, but you just had to enlighten them, to warp their minds, just as your own is warped. They hardly understand the natural functions of the body, let alone the unnatural."

She pouted, "I was just tryin' to get a laugh."

"Did you feel good when you got your laugh?"

"I never feel good."

Wretchedness pulled down the corners of her old-young mouth. She was baffling, rebellious, pitiful and frustrating. But any show of sympathy she would immediately interpret as a sign of weakness.

"Stand up," I said briskly in my best top-sergeant manner. She obeyed, her joints sagging in unwillingness.

"Why do you wear your clothes so skimpy? There's no shortage of material in the world."

"I'm just a growin' girl," she smirked.

"You didn't grow that much in two months. How many skirts do you have?"

"About five."

"All right. We're going to lengthen them. Every time you come down here, bring a couple of skirts along until we get all of your hems lowered."

"Why?" she challenged. "Nothin' wrong with my knees. Didn't God make all creation? And all He made was beautiful? So I'll show my beautiful knees. *If* you don't mind."

The girl was funny. A picture of a sultry red-head in slinky black evening gown entertaining at some smoke-filled night club passed briefly through my mind.

I gave her a brisk shove into my bedroom. "Take off your skirt and let out that hem. Here's my housecoat you can put on. When you're ready, I'll mark it for you."

Not for a minute could I let down my guard with that girl. A reasonable tone of voice she would defy; only sharp commands did she heed. I marked her hem and showed her how to make a blind stitch. She acted as if she had never held a needle before. Under her tight sweater lurked some tell-tale bulges.

"Do you have pins in all your straps?" I asked.

"Yeah. They break. I have to hold them some way."

I pretended I had never indulged in such slovenliness myself. "Miriam, that's *sloppy!* Use a needle and thread. It only takes a couple of minutes, and it's so much neater."

"I don't have any."

I handed her a spool of white thread and a packet of needles to keep in her room.

Bruce came in while she was in the bedroom, putting on her newly-lengthened skirt. Without realizing his presence, Miriam came back into the kitchen.

"It feels funny. Hope I don't look like an old maid," she remarked, and stopped, her eyes on Bruce. Her face paled. She seemed frightened. Bruce was tall, and in the low-ceilinged apartment, he appeared taller.

He smiled at her and joked, "How could a pretty young girl look like an old maid?"

She flushed and lowered her eyelids in something akin to demureness. I introduced them. Bruce offered,

"C'mon, Miriam, I'll drive you up to your dining hall."

"No, thanks. I can walk."

"It's dark. And you'll be late. This your coat?"

He held it for her. Judging from Miriam's awkward embarrassment, it was the first time a man had performed such a service for her. He held the outside door until she had passed through. A few minutes later, he was back.

"She didn't seem like such a wild kid," he remarked. "I think she's shy."

Shy? I could have laughed and cried at the same time.

A subtle change came over my classes. There was a danger in being too nice — seventh graders did not need friendly camaraderie from their teachers so much as they needed unflinching firmness. When I stopped accepting their flimsy excuses for unfinished homework, I began to get better performance, even from the good students. In the two months I had learned a very important lesson — good teaching demanded a great deal more than a college degree and a liking for young people.

Miriam returned on Thursday afternoon, a trifle less belligerent. I marked two more of her skirts, and watched while she hemmed them. Her tight sweaters had been shrunk deliberately — there was nothing I could do about them.

"Would your father send you money for clothes, Miriam?" I asked.

"He sends me five bucks a week.. There's nothin' to spend it on in this dump. I got about fifteen dollars in my drawer," she replied. Her voice was actually civil.

"I'll talk to your house mother. Maybe she'll let you ride over to Hampden with me on Saturday to shop for some clothes." A gleam of pleasure shone for an instant in her eye before she remembered to conceal it. "Okay."

I watched her red head bent over her skirt. It was straighter than straight, but of beautiful shade and texture.

"Miriam, do you wear your hair long to please your father?" I asked.

She guffawed loudly and humorlessly. "What does *he* care about my hair? No. I don't know what to do with it. At least this way it's out of my eyes."

"Your face is thin. It would be pretty if you framed your hair around it."

She looked up, almost shyly. "Could you — fix it like — yours?"

Flattered, but dubious, I replied, "My hair is curly, Miriam. It takes a special kind of cutting. Straight hair is really much more manageable, because you can make it do anything you wish. Let's try a shoulder bob."

She was most agreeable. Phyl, my best friend, had showed me how to do a simple trim, shaping the hair to the head. I borrowed large curlers and a hair dryer from my next door neighbor, and set Miriam's hair. When combed out, it made her look like a different girl. Bruce came in as she primped before the bathroom mirror.

She whirled and blanched as she heard his footstep.

"My word! What is this vision?" he teased, blinking his eyes as if the glare were too much for him. Miriam glowed.

I began to feel a glimmer of happiness in my experiment. Already the truculent girl had become more cooperative. She craved attention, and perhaps my interest in her appearance would be the first step in her long road to decent womanhood. I entertained no visions of miracle-working, for I knew my own impatience. But I prayed the Lord would use this time to draw Miriam into a knowledge of the joy a Christian life could offer.

Friday afternoon I popped into the house where some of the seventh grade girls lived to speak to Miriam's house mother. She readily granted permission. I suspected from her eagerness that she would have granted Miriam permission to go *anywhere,* as long as she was out of sight! One of the other girls was in the living room, waiting to play a record on the hi-fi set.

"Oh, Mrs. King," she bubbled, "are you going to Hampden tomorrow? Could I go along? I've been *dying* to buy myself a new sweater. My aunt sent the money ages ago. My skirt has this tan and aqua plaid, and if I could find a sweater to match it, it would be just perfect! Please?"

She clasped her hands under her chin in a gesture of appeal.

"Okay," I laughed. "Be ready at 8:00, Sue."

Perhaps Sue would strike up a friendship with Miriam. The daughter of missionaries to Africa, she was a gay, vivacious child, not at all awed by anyone, including teachers. Miriam claimed none of the girls liked her. Perhaps a morning with Sue would provide the basis for a budding friendship. I could only grasp at straws.

The morning began inauspiciously with a downpour of rain. I drove Bruce to his eight o'clock class so I could have the car, then swung across campus to the girls' house. Waiting on the front porch were, not two, but four girls.

Miriam's face was a study in dejection. "I thought we were going alone," she grumbled in accusation. She took the front seat while Sue and her friends climbed, chattering, into the back.

"Mrs. King, I hope you don't mind," Sue bubbled. She never just said anything — she always burst with a hundred and one bits of information. "Nancy and Faith wanted to do some shopping, too, and I couldn't call you on the phone, so I just knew it would be all right."

I tried to disguise my extreme annoyance with the girl. At her age, I would have been equally thoughtless.

Between thirteen and fifteen yawns a chasm bridged only by the passing of several stages of development. Nancy, Faith and Sue were well-behaved, innocuous girls. In Miriam's eyes, they were dodos. They sat in the back seat, giggling, talking in some teen code language, effectively excluding Miriam. By the time we reached Hampden, I could have cheerfully wrung their necks.

27

Yet we were saddled with them. This day, which was to have been Miriam's alone, nearly proved a disastrous fiasco.

The other three girls, after seeking my advice on colors, left us to shop elsewhere. We made arrangements to meet at the ice cream counter at ten-thirty. Miriam and I went together to the girl's department. Miriam displayed little interest in sweaters. Her manner become progressively more apathetic. Finally, to curb my impatience, I selected two for her. She had given me her money. By the time I had paid for the sweaters, Miriam had disappeared. I looked up and down the aisles. How a girl so tall could become so quickly invisible, was a mystery!

Fifteen minutes still remained before the other girls were to be at the ice cream counter. Confident that Miriam would return, I seized the opportunity to do some of my own shopping. After all, a fifteen-year-old should not get lost in a town the size of Hampden.

Sue, Faith and Nancy appeared at the ice cream counter promptly at ten-thirty. They ordered some concoction called an "awful-awful." As I watched them consume it, my stomach churned. They were sweet girls, all from secure, loving families. I knew why Miriam detested them.

By 11:00 she still had not reappeared. I suggested the girls wait in the car while I searched. Hampden was not large, but I did not know where to look. The clothing departments were not her chief interest. Books? Music? Art? Only one store held an art department, and no one had seen a girl fitting Miriam's description. By 11:30 I was reduced to taking quick glances into beer joints.

And then I found her — not in a beer joint, but a bowling alley. Her back to the door, she was leaning on a pin ball machine, her hips curved, her red locks hung over one shoulder. Even in what started out to be well-fitting clothing, she managed to intimate there was little left to conceal.

A young man in need of a shave was playing the machine next to hers. With a cigarette dangling from the corner of his mouth, he paused every now and then to take a swig out of a pop bottle. He was one of those workless wonders who populate recreation centers on a Saturday morning.

Miriam started when she saw me. Determined to brazen it through, she asked, "Is it time to go already? I didn't keep you waiting, did I?"

"Where's your coat?"

"Over there." She started toward the coat hooks along the

28

opposite wall. Beside the young man, she paused to whisper something low. He grinned, glanced at me, and went back to the serious business of his pinball machine.

Sometimes I wondered what a good thrashing would accomplish for a girl like Miriam. Nothing reached her. I tried to explain the danger of picking up strange men. She only mocked me with her pale eyes and sultry mouth. She had so far successfully blocked every attempt to reach her with friendship. She literally seemed hell-bent on her own destruction.

But when she came to the apartment Tuesday afternoon, her manner was fairly subdued. Sweet she would never be, but her new docility was encouraging. She had already taken out the hems of her last two skirts, and allowed me to mark them without undue rebuff. I had prayed earnestly for a time to touch her hardened surface; all the while I was conscious of deep weariness. Miriam's effect on me was that of a leech draining my energy.

She looked up from her sewing to observe, "Your husband—he's nice, isn't he? I wonder if a man will ever look at me like he looks at you."

"If you give your heart to the Lord to change, and to make a new creature of you, Miriam, it could happen. A Christ-centered life is the only way to begin a marriage. Love is a wonderful, awesome thing. Don't cheapen it with experimentation before you marry."

The mocking smile flitted across her mouth, but she gave no smart reply. For over an hour I talked with the girl, more frankly than I could have to my own sister. Pointing out God's repeated commands to refrain from all appearances of evil, I urged her to accept His offer of a free salvation — to let Him accomplish in her life what no one else could do. Her eyes shifted sideways at me, then back to the now-finished skirts. It was nearing five.

"Miriam," I asked, "will you pray with me?"

"You can," she said.

"Won't you?"

"No."

I bent my head and prayed aloud. When I raised my eyes, Miriam was staring out the window, only boredom showing in her face.

She flushed when Bruce came home. She had a crush on him, I realized. All to the good, if we could raise the girl's standards to realize that this was the kind of young man Christianity produced.

The mood of the evening, for the first time, was heavy — almost discontented. Miriam always depressed me; but the afternoon's session had given me a faint glimmer of hope. The gloom was not entirely in my mind. Bruce was restless and taciturn, seething with unspoken anger. Whatever bothered him, he did not want to discuss. I knew he was sensitive, and reluctant to admit it. Perhaps some incident with his lab partner? No. He didn't care enough for the fellow to be hurt by him. The professor's marking methods? Bruce was too mature to smart under unfairness to that extent.

Eventually, we went to bed. And in the morning, everything was right again.

Thursday noon at lunch, Bruce asked, "Is that girl coming here again today?"

"Yes. Why?"

"Tell her this is the last time. And send her home before dark. I'm tired of late dinners."

"Bruce, I might be making progress with her. At least she listened to me Tuesday when I talked to her about the Lord."

"Yeah?" He was unconvinced. He leaned across the table to take my hand in his. "Sandy, I wouldn't mind your helping her, but it's too much of a drain on you. You get too involved emotionally. You can't devote enough attention to your other duties."

"Why?" I asked, instantly defensive. "Has Mrs. Stibbe complained to you?" It wouldn't have been characteristic of my principal, for she was direct enough to tell a subordinate to her face if her performance were not satisfactory.

"No. Not that. I'm just tired of having that girl around. See her after class if you want to counsel with her."

His decisive tone bade me obey. It provided relief, for I was tired. What had started out as punishment for Miriam had proved more hardship on me!

But then, later in the day, I wondered if we were being too hasty. Something had upset Miriam. Her behavior was extraordinary, for she jumped at the slightest word. She had never been a soothing individual, but this nervousness was worse than her previous apathy. Half an hour before Bruce was due home, I said,

"Run along, Miriam. I guess you won't have to come back.

30

If you ever want to talk to someone, let me know. I'll help if I can. And please — stay out of trouble."

"Okay." She picked up her skirts and fled, without even a thank you. I felt like a mother abandoning her baby on someone's doorstep.

In class, I kept a close watch on Miriam. It became increasingly impossible to rouse even the faintest flicker of interest. Grammar *is* dull — I hated it as a student, and disliked it only slightly less as a teacher. But literature — there was not a book or author to kindle the girl's attention. *Treasure Island, The Yearling, Anne of Green Gables,* all bored her in equal measure. If she had shown some interest even in *Donald Duck,* I would have found cause for rejoicing. She failed every test, turned in no book reports. If my other students had performed as poorly, I would have seriously questioned my ability as a teacher.

Something was amiss. I felt it in the school corridors. The flutter of conversation which died as I passed a huddled group of girls. The tight-lipped smile from Mrs. Stibbe. The knowledgeable grins on the boys' faces. Even the unwonted hush as I entered the classroom. And when Miriam did not appear with English Seven-One, I knew whom it concerned.

All day I waited for word. There was a hastily-called faculty meeting. Since I was only hired on a temporary basis, I was not considered part of the faculty when it came to decision-making. The arrangement suited me fine, for I abhorred endless meetings with their endless talk. But today I was edgy. If Miriam were the subject of discussion, I wanted to be consulted. I remained longer in my classroom than necessary, correcting papers as an excuse.

Mrs. Stibbe stood in the doorway, her face more drawn than usual. "I thought you would be here, Mrs. King," she said in her gentle voice, as she approached my desk. She looked directly into my face before continuing,

"We have expelled Miriam McCartney, by unanimous decision. She will be leaving Harbrook as soon as her father can drive up to school."

Stunned, I asked weakly, "Can't you give her another chance?"

"No. The Academy is not a reform school, Mrs. King. Miriam McCartney is only one student out of two hundred and seventy three. We can't run the risk of corrupting others on the slim chance of helping her."

Mrs. Stibbe sat on one of the student's desks and told me the story. Miriam had sneaked out of her house Sunday evening, returning about six the next morning in a thoroughly disheveled state. She refused to say where she had been, or what she had done. Such things were not difficult to deduce. Even given the benefit of the doubt, the girl's flaunting of the rules was serious. She undermined authority and she was failing every subject. There was not one point in her favor. The faculty and staff had been patient, trying to overlook a great deal because of the girl's unhappy background. Miriam appeared incorrigible.

Still, I was disappointed. It seemed to me a Christian faculty in a Christian school should exercise more Christian grace. And they hadn't asked my opinion. Knowing how keenly interested in the girl I had been, they could have extended me at least the courtesy of a hearing. I wouldn't have changed the situation, but I could have served as the miserable girl's only champion. It was altogether a disillusioning experience.

Reluctantly, I trudged across campus for a final plea. Miriam was in her room, packing, her roommate nowhere in sight.

"Miriam," I began, trying to take her hands in mine, "I'm sorry."

She drew back, as if physical contact repulsed her. "Yeah, I suppose you are." She wrinkled her nose in distaste. "You're soft. And sort of dumb."

I took her blouses out of the suitcase and showed her how to fold them with a minimum of wrinkling. "It's too late to have you re-instated, Miriam, but it's not too late to accept the Lord as your Saviour. Will you?"

She peered into the mirror, resting her elbows on the bureau. "D'you think I would look good in green eye shadow?"

"Miriam! Will you listen to me? This may be your last chance, your last contact with the Gospel!"

She straightened from the mirror, her pale eyes narrowing to blue slits. "Don't worry about me, Mrs. King. You — you're good, so you'll be all right. I'm bad, and I'll get along fine, too. It's the ones in between who run into trouble."

I recalled Steinbeck's *East of Eden*. I had always considered his characterization of Cathy too extreme, too thoroughly dedicated to evil, too wholly soul-less. Yet, looking at this tall girl with the red-gold hair and old-young mouth, I wondered.

"Bruce, she's so young!" I cried in his arms that night. "If only we had tried a little harder! She can't be as tough as she

32

pretends! If the school would only give her another chance! Someone *has* to reach her!"

He shook my shoulder roughly. "Sandy! That girl's rotten to the core! Do you know the last time I took her home, I actually had to slap her down to make her get out of the car!"

I couldn't believe him. That night – he had been distraught. But still——!

"Sandy," he went on in a calmer voice, "I've met bold women in my life. Even they weren't like Miriam. Get her out of your mind. The Lord expects us to help others, but He doesn't expect us to be complete idiots while we're about it!"

And perhaps they were all right, and I was all wrong. It did not seem to me any creature of God could be entirely beyond redemption. Yet even God in His omnipotence, did not choose to work a miracle where none was sought. More amoral than immoral, Miriam had made her choice. What would become of her? I never knew.

CHAPTER THREE

The experience had bruised me. I blamed the school for inflexibility, but more I blamed myself. I had been concerned for the girl's welfare, but I had not really liked her. Even a puppy can sense distaste, and Miriam's sensitivity far exceeded a puppy's. She could not respond to anything less than a wholehearted love. The failure was mine, and the taste of ashes lay in my mouth.

The long Thanksgiving weekend brought an easing of heartache, for Jack and Jane Brownell, our college roommates, arrived late Wednesday evening to spend three days with us. The Brownells had been married a week before we had. During our final year, they had steadied our turbulent romance. Both were easygoing, placid individuals, but where Jane tended to be over-serious, Jack provided the gentle humor so necessary to everyday life. They were good for us; we were good for them. All through the

33

passing years, we never found a couple we both so thoroughly enjoyed.

Our next door neighbors, the Crockets, had gone to her mother's for the Thanksgiving weekend, leaving their apartment free for our guests.

For three days we laughed and ate and played games and exchanged gossip like Civil War veterans. Jack reported for a small town newspaper, with bright prospects for moving to news editor's position. Jane worked as assistant in the public library, among the books she so dearly loved. They were happy in their work, satisfied in their love.

Far into the night we exchanged our views on every conceivable subject, from the presidential campaign to Harbrook's doctrinal standards. In the daylight, too weary for serious discussion, we joked in a lighter vein.

And suddenly, it came to me – I had been lonesome! Right in the middle of a bustling campus of one thousand souls, with a husband who adored me, I had been lonesome! More than I knew, I had missed Jane and Dotty and Ramona and Louise and all the other girls who had comprised our college circle. Whatever can be said about it, marriage talk wasn't the same as girl talk. There were whole areas of conversation in which I could not interest Bruce – surely he felt the same about me – but Jane fulfilled the need for feminine chatter. We confided in delicious enjoyment of one another, free of the daily wear and tear for a short time. Perhaps in that weekend we drew closer than we had been in the four years we had roomed together.

Jane's plain face had filled out with contentment. Her light brown hair was arranged becomingly, and she had grown almost pretty. Jack had gained ten pounds. On an already chubby figure, it was too much. When Jane admonished him about over-eating, he only turned a deaf ear and helped himself to seconds. Nothing ruffled his imperturbable calm, nor roiled his keen mind. Their relationship was quite different from ours, though I could not exactly state in what way. They had never been so blindly in love as we, and yet, they were perfect for each other.

Nothing marred their three-day visit. But, when they pulled out of the drive in their shabby sedan, Bruce pulled me into his arms to murmur, "It's good to be alone again."

"You know, I think Jack is saying the same thing to Jane – it's good to be alone again."

And it was. We were beginning to feel like old married people, with a premium on our privacy.

School teaching settled into a routine. Though I missed the challenge of Miriam, class proved considerably easier to conduct without her. My work was no longer the nerve-wracking chore of the previous months.

In the dark winter mornings when the alarm sounded, I struggled against the drug of warm sleep, finally managing to get myself out of bed. Bruce never did more than flutter an eyelash until the smell of percolating coffee struck his nostrils. I did not see why I *always* had to be the first one up, but it seemed one of those little marital snags I could not resolve. If I'd waited for him to move, I would have been late for class. It dawned on me that a school teacher's lot was more demanding than a student's. I had been prone to believe some college professors were a trifle sadistic in their assignments. Now I regretted my years of moaning under the burden.

In the years we had spent in upper New York, we came to expect our share of snow. That year we received double measure, pressed down, and overflowing. Every morning, another six or eight or one or two inches had fallen. The unimportant road to the married students' barracks was the last to be plowed, which meant that more mornings than not we would plod through the drifts, up the hill to our respective destinations. Bruce's feet were bigger than mine, but his legs were also longer. When he forgot and took a stride too long, my feet landed in deep snow, and cold wet crystals filled my boots.

"Bruce!" I yelled. "Take smaller steps!"

"Why don't you grow longer legs?" he retorted.

"Now I know the honeymoon is over," I whimpered in good imitation of those soap operas I used to love. "Before we were married, you never found fault with my legs."

"Yeah, I know," he agreed. "If I really loved you, I'd carry you, but it's pretty hard to do with all these books in my arms."

By this time we had reached the plowed road which led up the hill to the education buildings. I paused to pour out the melted snow from my boots.

All about us, white crystalline jewels covered the ground, the hills, the trees. Dazzling morning sunshine glinted off the new brightness. Wind had created uneven patterns of drifts peaking in gentle artistry. The white and black guard posts were military sentinels at strict attention, capped by rounded white tufts of caps. Bird patterns across the snow were the only signs

35

of life from meadow to mountain. Our mood shifted from jocular to awesome in an instant.

" 'The heavens declare the glory of God,
And the firmament showeth His handiwork.'
Bruce, how could anyone think — all this — just happened?"

"On paper they could. Not when they look about them."

Sheltered from the wind, now, we trudged up the hill, no longer annoyed at nature's bountiful distribution of snow. It had been meant for our eyes, not for our feet!

Home for Christmas! Lest I sound like a sentimentalist from a Grandma Moses landscape, I will refrain from eulogizing the comforts, warmth and love those three words embrace. Again, my parents sent us gas money for travel home. They also sent a check to my brother, Ray, to bring him and his new wife up from Texas. For the first time in a year, we were a complete family, with two full-grown additions.

Marriage had matured Ray, bringing out the resemblance to our father even stronger than in the years past. He was the only brilliant one in the family, with a scholastic record worth noting. Intent on his theological course, he planned to earn his doctorate in another year. Serious-minded, but gentle, there was an undercurrent of strain in Ray apparent from the first greeting. I caught an exchange of glances between Mother and Dad which told me I was not imagining everything.

Ann was an enigma. Last Christmas, in the flush of early love, Ray had described Ann in glowing affection. I had pictured some model of Christian womanhood, bustling, efficient, cheerful and devout. Ann was none of these. She complained of the New England cold in a high-pitched Texas whine. Most of the day she huddled near the radiator, wrapped in an old-fashioned quilt, reading, reading. Her material ran more to slick magazines than anything of great merit. She did not come into the kitchen to help with meals or dishes. She ate very sparingly of Mother's delicious meals, covering everything with ketchup as if this were the only way she could render it palatable. Though Southerners are supposed to possess great charm, she rarely said anything complimentary about anyone or anything. She could listen to Carol's rendition of Rachmaninoff's *Prelude* with no comment. Ronnie, a cute teenager with a store of clever wisecracks, she ignored almost completely. Ray and Bruce and I all made efforts to draw her into the family circle, but Ann resisted any attempt at friendship with a thinly disguised boredom.

Still, she was my favorite brother's wife. For his sake, if for nothing else, I determined to break through the veneer of subtle hostility. Whatever had happened in the seven months of their marriage, this surely could not be the girl my brother had fallen in love with! As if on the spur of the moment, I invited Ann to walk over to Phyl Howland's with me to see Phyl's new baby.

Reluctantly, Ann dragged herself off the sofa and garbed herself suitably for an expedition to the Arctic. After donning sweater, kerchief, hooded jacket, slacks, boots and two pair of mittens, she stood uncertainly in the back doorway. Outside, a neighbor's dog barked his greeting. The air was brisk and bright — a perfect New England day.

"Oh, I'm scared of dogs," she said.

"That's just Rusty," I breezed in my off-hand manner. "He's half a century old, and couldn't hurt a fly. Come on."

She held back. "Are you sure? Suppose there are others on the way?"

Phyl lived four blocks from us, and there were likely to be several dozen dogs in the intervening distance, for Bartlett enforced no law on pet-tying. From a corner of the back porch, I picked up an old cane Ronnie had discarded long ago after discovery in the town dump.

"Here, I'll protect you," I half teased, as I pulled Ann out the door. Still reluctant, she walked timidly beside me, cowering as we passed old Rusty. The entire incident seemed such an act. Ann did not look like a clinging vine. If she had been frail of build, and delicate of feature, I could have understood her behavior better. Instead, she was a strapping girl, taller than I, with broad shoulders and wide hips. Occasionally, from her light eyes a flash of humor would glint, only to be quickly suppressed. Ann behaved like nothing more than a petulant child determined to punish her family. In this case, the family had no idea what it was being punished for!

Without mishap, we arrived at Phyl's apartment. The morning sunbeams glinted through her polished windows, onto the marbleized tile. Her kitchen was spotless, though somewhat disarrayed with the accouterments of the baby's bath.

Since time began, Phyl had been my best friend We had laughed together, cried together, fallen in and out of love together. Now married and the mother of a month-old boy, Phyl couldn't wait to show him off. She bubbled over with delight at every movement of his tiny fist. His cry was the sweetest, his smile the most endearing, his eyes the brightest, his head the best-shaped of any baby on this earth. Even Ann was forced to smile at Phyl's ecstatic rhapsody. Across his bathinette we exchanged amused grins. Given enough time, I thought we might even be friends. But on the way home, she retreated once more into her cocoon.

Ten days, from the beginning, seems a long time. We plan long, confidential chats with each member of the family, think we'll see everyone we know, attend all the Christmas functions given. But time races so quickly that we accomplish less than half of what we plan. I wanted to talk with Ray, but somehow, in the first few days, we never managed to be alone.

Toward the end of the first week, I took the car to do some shopping for Mother. Ray came around from shovelling snow in the driveway and hopped in the other side. We valued what time we had together, for our friendship ran deep.

People not understanding the New England temperament call us abrupt. This may be so, but at least we don't waste time in "nicey-nice" talk which means absolutely nothing. Ray had something on his mind, and he said it.

"I was hoping you and Ann would be good friends," he said in his direct manner, as he watched the expression on my face. Rather than accusing, his voice seemed more observant. We had never been less than honest with each other. I stopped for a red light, and turned to my brother.

"I hoped so, too, Ray. She doesn't give me much of a chance."

"I know. She — Ann has two sides to her. If it didn't sound so much like a serious psychiatric problem, I'd say she has a split personality. She can be lovely, fun-filled, hard-working. That's what I saw before we were married." His voice trailed.

"Ann seems to be afraid of new things, Sandy. Living out on a ranch like she did, she rarely met anyone new, never heard an outsider's viewpoint. When we moved to town so I could be closer to school, she began to show her shyness. She didn't want to come here for Christmas. She was afraid to meet the family — especially you."

"Me?" The light changed. I shifted gears and drove on, past our old school house, empty now for Christmas vacation and on up to the shopping center. "Why would she be afraid of me?"

"She thinks you're too smart and too pretty for her to compete."

"But I'm not smart or pretty! Now that she's met me, she knows that. Why should she want to *compete* with me? I'm not your former girlfriend."

"I don't know, Sis. Her love is — well, Bruce's love for you is somewhat possessive." He was searching for words. "But Ann's for me is — more — *ob*sessive. She — maybe she's afraid that if I love someone else, there will be less love for her."

"She thinks love divides instead of multiplies?"

He looked at me, surprised. "Yes, that's it. And now she's pregnant——"

"I didn't know that. Does Mother?"

"Ann doesn't want anyone to know. She's afraid to have a baby, Sandy. She's afraid I'll love the baby more than her. She spends her days in fear and her night in tears."

I found a parking place and pulled to a stop.

"You're asking me to help?"

"I'm asking you to understand."

My poor, wonderful big brother! What had he gotten into? With a limitless future of opportunities open before him, he had been saddled with this neurotic bundle of female nerves. I wanted to declare categorically,

"She's sick, Ray. Take her to a Christian psychiatrist before she gets worse."

He read my thoughts. In misery, he related,

"We had a bad time of it a few weeks ago. After I had written saying we were coming home for Christmas, Ann decided definitely she was pregnant. She said she didn't want to come north with me, that I should just come on by myself and leave her to spend Christmas all alone. She went into hysterics, but it wasn't the first time. Other times she's snapped out of her sulks in a day or two. Now she's punishing me for insisting she come to Bartlett. She'd already made up her mind she didn't like Yankees, that they were all unfriendly."

"Why? She married one."

"Yes." Ray sighed, drumming his fingers nervously on the door handle. The day had turned gloomy and dark. A few stray snowflakes drifted uncertainly on to the windshield, to melt into tiny rivulets and stream down the hood.

"Is she a Christian, Ray?"

"Oh, sure. In her town, everyone's a Christian. It's all they hear in church — salvation. Sunday morning, Sunday night, Wednesday prayer meeting. There's no food for the maturing Christian, no demands made on his life. Just be saved and go around singing 'When the Roll Is Called Up Yonder I'll Be There.' "

I was startled. Never had Ray played the role of bitter disillusionment. He turned to face me, his eyes suddenly filled with tears.

"Sandy, did you ever doubt God? I can't talk to anyone! She stifles me! I can't breathe! I can't study! She follows me around all the time I'm home, making little noises to distract. She thinks she has to be the very *center* of my every thought. She doesn't want me to finish my schooling. She wants me to go work on her father's ranch, where nothing is new, where everything is familiar to her."

Ray hadn't meant to pour all this out. Once loosed, the torrent of words could not stop. His first sentence, more than the rest, alarmed me.

"Ray, are you doubting God?"

"Yes," he said. "I am. When things were so tough for you last year, I prayed, and I *knew* the Lord's will would be worked out for you. I can't get any assurance for myself. Sandy! Where did I go wrong? I didn't step into marriage blindly. I prayed about it, long before I ever asked Ann to marry me. She was so different then! She seemed to have all the qualities a man could want in a wife."

From my vast inexperience, I suggested weakly, "Pregnancy does strange things to people. Maybe if you tried babying her——"

"I've babied her. She laps it up and begs for more. The trouble is exaggerated with pregnancy, but it was there long before. I know Ann's problems go back several years — she was responsible for the accident that killed her mother — but, Sandy, will this poison us all our lives? Are we to live in perpetual fear? Shall we shut ourselves off from all of life, and go vegetate on a lonely ranch? I'm not a rancher, or a farmer. I could be a good teacher!"

I put my hand on his, and stared directly into his eyes. It was like looking into a mirror, so much were they like mine.

"Ray," I began very deliberately, "I don't know much. But I know this. God hears when we pray. He answers when we ask. You and Ann will come through this, and it will be as if it never happened." My voice was so sure I could scarcely recognize it for my own. Exactly what made me so positive, I could never say. Ray was too good, too capable, to be cast on the dung-heap of a wife's neurosis. Ann would straighten out. She had to!

Too wrought up by our mutual sensitivity, neither of us could pray aloud. We bowed our heads for a moment, then opened our doors to begin Mother's shopping.

In the store, I tried to think of something that would please Ann.

"What does Ann do well, Ray?"

"She's a superb cook. That's all she cares about—her kitchen."

"Why don't we buy the ingredients and suggest she cook us a Texan meal?"

"We can try." He didn't sound too enthusiastic. Already he regretted his confidence in the car. He had overstepped the bounds of loyalty to his wife. In order not to antagonize him, I knew I must tread easy in any reference to Ann.

We purchased corn meal, salt pork, blackeyed peas and ham, hoping we'd have the necessary foods for Ann's style of cooking. All through the store, as I pulled cans of food and frozen packages from the shelves, I pondered the problem, almost sick with grief for my brother. Where had he missed God's guidance? When His children pray for help, does the Lord allow them to make mistakes? Or did some of the fault lie in Ray? In family troubles, feelings rule reason. The possibility existed, however, that the characteristics we Marshalls found admirable irritated Ann.

We stowed our purchases in the back seat, and got into the car again. I inserted the key in the ignition; then, before turning it, I looked at Ray closely. His mouth was drawn, and his skin very pale. His revelation had taken more out of him than he had anticipated.

"Ray," I said somewhat timidly, "I know you want to be through with the subject, but I want to say something. And then I promise never to bring it up again. Did it ever occur to you, that, living with Mother and Dad, we've been very pampered? They seem to get along in such close harmony, that we aren't prepared for troubles in our own lives. But Ray, we weren't around the first year of their marriage. Maybe they had a lot of adjusting to do that we never heard about."

Ray looked at me, a faint smile on his colorless lips. I knew the idea had never occurred to him. "Maybe you're right, Sis. Maybe I expected too much of marriage. But a man should expect some companionship in thought! Ann's idea of interesting conversation is how her new kitchen curtains look!"

Through the dark forest, a little light began to glimmer. "And what do you want to talk about — Niebuhr and Tillich?"

"Yes — or even current events! Do you know what she said the first week we were married?" He took on an imitation of a Southern drawl. " 'Ah didn't know any *nice* people were Republicans!' "

I threw back my head and laughed. Poor Ray, with his passion for discussion, his craving for broad understanding. He had no patience with pettiness, in people or outlook.

"Ray!" I pled. "Be careful! You must not make Ann feel inferior. Every family doesn't talk like we do around the table. Women aren't particularly interested in politics or theology."

"Aren't you?"

"No. And when Bruce looks up from his studies, all excited about the vertebrate structure of the sub-human primate, I put my mind in neutral. He can talk about it if he wants to, but I don't have to listen to him! Ann doesn't work, does she?"

"No."

"Then she has nothing to fill her mind but her home. Be patient, Ray. After the baby comes, you'll have a mutual interest. Look at Phyl and Jim — she said they squabbled all the time before the baby was born, and now they haven't had a fight since."

"Oh, Ann and I don't fight! We wear each other out."

"Try building her up, Ray. Maybe it's something you'll have to do all your life, but it would be worth it if you secured a good home."

He sighed. "I'll try, Sandy. I only wish I thought kitchen curtains were interesting!"

"She makes them for you. She cooks for you. She needs your appreciation. And I'll bet if you stopped using your high-flown theological terms and brought your discussion down to a lay person's level, she'd become more interested in your studies. Men are interested in ideas and things. Women are interested in people. Somewhere, through the maze, we have to find a common ground. It isn't always easy."

"Now, that's the understatement of the year!" Ray laughed lightly. His gloom somewhat dispelled, he talked of other things on the way home.

We had taken most of the morning for a very short shopping list.

"What happened?" Mother asked, when Ray brought in the groceries. "Were the lines so long on a Thursday?"

"No. We were hashing over old times," I explained.

Through the years of growing up, I had always been my father's daughter, genuinely preferring his company to my mother's. Gradually, the relationship was changing, for we had many things to talk about now — new recipes, young people in the church, Carol and Ronnie's development. She seemed to possess some extrasensory perception in problems of the heart, for it took little explanation for her to grasp the feel of a situation, even though all details were not clear.

Later, from my post at the kitchen sink, I heard Ray suggest to Ann that she teach Mother and me how to make real Southern corn bread. She came hesitantly into the kitchen, as if treading on hostile territory.

"Hey, Mom," Ray said. "I'm hungry for some of Ann's cooking. Why don't you let her get supper for tonight?"

Mother dropped her knife in surprise, completely at a loss. She recovered quickly with a smile.

"Fine, if you're sure you don't mind, Ann. I wanted to take a Christmas basket to a sick friend. If you take charge, I won't have to hurry back."

Ann was no nitwit. She must have seen through the ruse. But she must have been tired of her sulks, and compliance gave her the only gracious excuse for dropping them.

Black-eyed peas had never sounded tremendously enticing to me. But, cooked with Ann's special style of seasoning, they were delicious. Her ham, glazed with brown sugar and mustard and whole cloves, was a gourmet's delight. A flush of pleasure reddened her cheeks at the family's compliments, for she knew we were sincere.

Cooking one meal for her in-laws was not a cure-all for Ann's deep-rooted insecurity. She craved praise as a baby craves love. Perhaps it was a bit of the same thing. In some areas of emotion, she was still an infant. But with patience and prayer, impediments to their happiness could dwindle to a mere memory. As Ann grew in her Christian life, she would come to realize that fear is an insult to God. Provided, of course, that she did not allow it to become a pattern for her development.

Carol had blossomed considerably since attending the Conservatory of Music. Nothing hastens the maturing process so quickly as a break from home. Though still shy, she could carry on easy conversation without blushing. All the way from Boston a young man came to call. More than the boy himself, she enjoyed the interest this stirred, for Carol had been the truest kind of wallflower. Even the incorrigible Ronnie managed to keep his teasing down to a minimum until they had departed for their date.

"Is it lonely, Mother, seeing your children grow up and away from you?" I asked. The expression in her eyes had been wistful. She turned to look at me full-face.

"Yes and no. It's heart-rending to realize they no longer need your advice on everything. But it's very satisfying to know they all love the Lord, and to realize that without the proper home, they probably wouldn't be Christians. If I've done nothing else, I know I've taught my children right."

"Do you miss the noise and confusion?"

"Some. But we can't hold Time back, and I don't think we'd really want to. Now we're looking forward to our first grandchild."

"Did Ray tell you?"

"Ann did. She can be very sweet, Sandy. She wants me to come to Texas to help when the baby comes."

"Do you think you will?"

"I'd like to. I think I could help her over the hump. You've never experienced fear, Sandy. It can be a most troublesome emotion. We can tell people to trust the Lord, but it isn't always easy for them to do. Ann needs a lot of teaching."

I squeezed my mother's soft arm. "I can't think of a better teacher."

CHAPTER FOUR

Three and a half weeks remained at Harbrook. They were anti-climactic. We could not believe it was time now to leave our lovely little college, scene of our greatest spiritual battles, site of the turning point in our lives. Our finest friends, our careers, had been chosen here. We could not leave without a great wrenching of the heart.

Though it would have been much easier to steal away without uttering one good-by, we went through the ritual of rending farewells. Our professors, Mrs. Stibbe, my seventh grade students, how we loved them all! To them, we were only another young couple, launching into God's service. To us, it was the closing of a very tender period. When the moment came, it seemed we could not bear it.

We packed the car to the gills the night before our departure, with barely space enough to seat ourselves. Our apartment had been furnished; we owned nothing big. Still, it seemed the supply of "little" things was endless. Our next door neighbors gave us breakfast early in the dawn of a gloomy January morning, and we were on our way.

It was a four-hour trip to Sheldon. We hoped to make it before noon, locate a furnished apartment and be settled by nightfall. Almost any kind of human habitation would do, for we had no funds to indulge a sense of beauty.

The prospect of life in Sheldon filled me with dread anticipation. Gone would be the warmth and friendliness of both Bartlett and Harbrook. The disinterest of a large city threatened to overwhelm me. We would have no friends, no family to bolster our spirits. More than ever we would need each other, and the Lord.

Earlier, I had timidly suggested that Bruce apply for entrance to other medical schools, for Sheldon was his home town. Disowned by his uncle, ignored by his brother, Bruce might discover the proximity to scenes of his childhood a source of discomfort. But Sheldon University rated the best medical training in the state. Since he had already been accepted there, Bruce had no urge to change. We would live in Sheldon, King family or no.

As we drove farther south, the clouds showed their sympathy with my dismal mood by pouring out their tears. The ironing board, packed in the back on my side, kept slipping forward to bump the back of my head. The egg sandwiches I had packed the night before, were soggy by noon. And then, less than fifty miles from Sheldon, the car began to clack. For so long it had been a trusted friend that we couldn't believe it would betray us in our hour of need. Bruce just managed to pull into a garage before it quit altogether.

We had to wait a half hour before the station attendant could find a berth for the car in his unheated garage. He opened the hood, muttering a few wise remarks dealing with fan belts, carburetors and cracked engine heads.

"Ya oughta trade this heap in while the market's still high," he confided to Bruce. "I can give ya a real good deal on that little Chevy over there."

We never even glanced at his little Chevy.

"Thanks. Can't you just get this one going?" asked Bruce.

"Yeah, I could, but I don't advise it. Ya need a complete overhaul. The car's six years old. Ya'd do better to trade it in on a newer one."

"Well, my name isn't Daddy Warbucks," said Bruce. "And I'd just as soon keep this car till it falls apart."

"Okay. It won't be long," our cheerful friend informed us.

He was the only person in the station. He would work a minute, then leave to fill a car with gas, come back to us, return to tend another customer, make change, exchange sage comments on the weather, return and work a few more minutes. Bruce and I stamped our feet in the damp cold, trying to ignore the passage of time. At this rate, we wouldn't have much time left for apartment hunting. And we couldn't afford a night in a motel!

Eventually, shortly after two, the car was running once again. We parted company with twenty-three dollars and eighty-two cents, and with a little prayer, we were off.

Sheldon was many cities in one. When I had visited Bruce's family the spring before, we saw the city of wealth and culture, with architectural beauty and broad, green lawns. Today we turned to another section, where tenements crowded anxiously together in self-defense. Drab streets lined with telephone poles and litter baskets drenched in the winter rain ran block after block. We could not look at each other, for we feared the hopelessness in the other's eyes.

At the first drugstore, we purchased a newspaper to search the want ads for an apartment. I had looked forward to househunting, to poking around in other people's closets. We never got that far. Rents started at seventy-five dollars a month, and skyrocketed upward. We had asked the Lord for a two-room apartment for not more than sixty. On a teacher's salary, I knew we could afford no more. But no one in Sheldon had any heart for struggling young students.

It was nearly six when we saw it. A driving rain had slowed our progress, and we were merely creeping along, when suddenly, in the window of a dreary corner store on Prospect Street, there was a sign. "Furnished Apartment for Rent. $60." Without even looking at it, we knew we'd found our home.

A little bell tinkled as we entered the store to inquire.

"It's six o'clock. Store's closed," grunted the woman behind the counter.

She was the perfect specimen of the original slob. Malevolent gray eyes peered suspiciously out of the wrinkled orb that was her face. A series of double chins oozed heavily over her dark wool cardigan. Thick cotton stockings, rolled at the knees and wrinkled at the ankles, covered the biggest legs I ever saw. She must have weighed close to three hundred pounds. When she moved, it was with the ponderous grace of a pachyderm. Even to the shape of her eyes, she could have been a close relative to that family.

"We came to ask about the apartment."

There was no visible change in her demeanor. "Upstairs. First door on the left. Here's the key. You can look at it yourselves."

The peculiar odor of stale foods and unwashed woodwork associated with tenements struck our nostrils as we opened the door into the hallway. We found the light switch, hanging from a thin string in the center of a very dark, very narrow hallway. A shutter creaked in the wind. All it needed was eerie voices calling dimly through the walls to complete the picture of the House on Haunted Hill.

Surprisingly, the apartment was clean. But dark! And gloomy! I shuddered. Bruce squeezed my arm comfortingly, and we began our tour of inspection. It didn't take long. The living room was all out of proportion to the rest of the layout. It was so large the couch and table and chairs seemed lonesome. Only a cracked blue linoleum rug covered the painted floor. The windows were high and small, as if in a basement apartment. I would have had to stand on a chair to see out of them.

"Why do you suppose the windows are like that?"

Bruce shrugged. "So no one can look in, I guess."

"On the second story?"

"Maybe the neighborhood is plagued with giants."

"Maybe she bought the windows at auction. See? They're not even the same size."

"I think she has the welfare of her tenants in mind. We won't need any shades, and not much curtain material."

The kitchen wasn't really a separate room — more like an alcove. The stove was a two-burner hot plate, with a sort of metal box which fitted over the burners when the lady of the house wanted to bake. Heaven help her if she decided to bake and boil at the same time! The refrigerator held freezing space big enough for one tray of ice cubes, no more. Over the sink hung a mirror, somewhat warped. It was the only faucet in the place, for the bathroom contained no washbowl.

The bedroom was no better. A large double bed nearly filled it to capacity, but our hostess had also managed to squeeze into it a dresser with three sticking drawers and a cardboard wardrobe in lieu of a closet. The bed was a metal affair, with flecks of paint peeling off the rounded slats of the headboard. Dan Cupid grinned sickeningly at us from his frame in the center of the wall. A previous tenant of artistic bent had pencilled in three widely-spaced teeth, giving the great messenger of love a slightly evil expression, as if he knew all the traps he could spring on his unsuspecting victims.

Bruce flopped on the bed, presumably to test the comfort, actually to rest his aching feet. "The mattress isn't lumpy," he conceded cheerfully.

"And it's only sixty dollars a month. Nothing else has been so cheap."

"You always like to go camping. We could pretend we were roughing it year round."

"Pretend!" I sagged down beside him. "And it's only ten minute's walk to the campus."

"If you run."

It was late. We were hungry, and very, very footsore. I looked around once more, trying not to mind the awful gray walls and varnished woodwork.

"Who do you suppose her interior decorator is?" I asked, coming once more into the bedroom, where Bruce still lay.

"Joe, the junk dealer," he murmured from beneath his arm, bent to shield his eyes from the 60 watt glare of the unshaded bulb.

"No. I think she goes farther than that. Sam, the Scavenger."

"Maybe we could cultivate his acquaintance, too. You never know what these contacts can mean to you."

In a wave of giggles approaching hysteria, I collapsed on the bed beside him. "Shall we take it?"

"We could always go to a motel for the night and look again in the morning."

"I don't think we'll find anything so cheap and so near your campus."

"What would my uncle think if he knew I was bringing you to a dump like this?" It was the first time in many months that Bruce had so much as mentioned his uncle. I thought it a healthy sign.

"I think it would give him great satisfaction. He could say 'I told you so' to his heart's content."

"Well, we could rent it for a month and that would give us time to get our bearings."

But it proved not to be so easy. Mrs. Ajarian, who waited for us at the bottom of the stairway, was not about to let us out of her grasp.

"One month's rent in advance, and sign a lease for six months," she demanded.

"Six months!" we echoed in unison.

She was adamant, and we were dead tired. Bruce sighed.

We moved in that night. Bruce carried in the box with my pans and silverware, I bought a pound of hamburger from Mrs. Ajarian, and cooked a hasty meal while Bruce unloaded the car.

We were nearly finished when a knock sounded on the door. From his place at the table, Bruce leaned back to open it. A policeman stepped inside. In a pleasant voice he said,

"Mrs. Ajarian says that's your car parked out front. Better move it, son. Ten minutes parking only on this street."

In consternation, Bruce stared at him. "Even for people who live here? Where will I park it?"

"There's a lot three blocks west. I think they give special rates to residents. But you better get it out of the way. I should have ticketed you a half hour ago."

I dashed through the pile of clothes on the bed to find Bruce's raincoat. Everything was a mess, and of course, the raincoat was the last thing I could lay my hands on. By the time I discovered it, Bruce had already left.

Twenty minutes later, dripping wet and irritable, he returned.

"Come on, sit down," I said. "The coffee's still hot." He tossed his wet jacket over the back of the room's only spare chair and sat down.

"Four fifty a week to park the car in that lot," he grumbled. "Some town!"

He said it. *I* wouldn't have dared.

This was our introduction to the fair city of Sheldon.

In the morning the sun was shining. We had slept well. The two-burner hot plate, though slow, worked. And life seemed not quite so glum. Bruce helped me straighten our belongings, then left for campus to have a look around. The gray walls and high ceilings were getting on his nerves. He left me alone to cope.

Nothing challenges a woman more than an impossible room in which to work a miracle. I need not fear ruining anything, for the room could not have been worse. Therefore, anything else was an improvement. It happened that two identical red and white checked tablecloths had been given us for wedding gifts. One I draped kitty corner over the drop leaf table. The other I cut into four strips, hemmed them by hand, and hung them on the spring-type curtain rods at the small windows. A plaid red-black-and-tan bedspread served as slip-cover for the dingy studio couch. Two small throw rugs covered the worst of the worn spots in the blue linoleum. Then, with a hammer and nails borrowed from Mrs. Ajarian, I hung two gay kitchen lamps on the walls. Suddenly, our apartment became fit for human habitation. I stepped out into the hall, closed the door for a minute, then stepped back in. It was lovely.

The bedroom was not so easy. It was so crowded, I had to sit on the bed in order to open the drawers. I sprawled on the bed and planned through half-closed lids. If the wardrobe were moved into the living room, we could put the dresser in its place, and both of us would be able to breathe at once. What about the solitary window? I hadn't anything to soften its harsh bareness. Our white chenille bedspread was lovely, but it added no color to this drab cell. It needed — what? Pink would be pretty, but Bruce preferred blue. What did I own that was blue, and would give me enough material for two lengths of curtain and a valance? I did not dare spend any money until I had a job, and even on a teacher's salary, we would be cutting close corners.

My problem was still unsolved when Bruce returned for a late lunch. He poked his head in, looked around, and grinned.

"Pardon me, madam, I'm looking for a Mrs. King. She lives in a run-down, ugly gray apartment. Would you happen to know her?"

Realizing that my hair had not been combed since seven o'clock that morning, I stretched my arms in mock melodrama. "I am she!" I gasped. "Haggard and worn, but I am Mrs. King. Don't you recognize me?"

He pulled up from a long kiss. "I recognize you, but not your room. Sandy, you're a genius. I couldn't believe this place could be so cozy!"

"Practically a mansion," I agreed. "Come eat your sandwich. I need your help with the bedroom afterwards."

Very willingly, he put his shoulder to the task of moving out the clumsy wardrobe. We placed it just outside the bedroom door, making it serve as a divider, for the living room was much too large, and the bedroom much too small. With the dresser shoved into the other corner, it now became almost habitable. Some paint on its apple-green surface would improve it considerably.

Panting, I asked, "But what about the curtains?"

"What about them? my husband asked. "I don't see any."

"That's just it. None of my summer skirts has enough material."

Bruce blinked. "Sounds like a *non sequitur* to me. Is there a connection?"

"To make the curtains out of! I used a tablecloth for the living room windows, but I haven't anything for the bedroom."

All of a sudden, it loomed as a huge problem which *had* to be solved that instant. I sank on the bed, near tears.

Bruce leaned against the doorjamb, deep in thought. "Let's see what I have," he said.

A second later I heard the lock in his trunk snap open. It had been filled with his belongings when he left his uncle's home last spring. I had never paid attention to its contents. After a moment of rummaging, Bruce came back into the bedroom, holding up a huge something in bright, shimmery stripes.

"How about this, Sandy? It's big enough for a tent."

I sat up. "What is it?"

He chuckled. "The head of Men's Wear in Uncle Larry's store stocked some of these 'Arabian robes' one year as a gimmick. They didn't sell, so Uncle Larry gave Don and me each one."

I swung my feet over the edge of the bed. "Oh, put it on, Bruce. Isn't it pretty? Just like Joseph's coat."

"I never saw his coat, but I'll take your word for it." He tied the bright pink sash about his middle and strutted as best he could in the limited space our boudoir offered.

I reached to feel the fabric. The sash was smooth satin, while the robe was silk taffeta in various shades of blue, lightened by thin stripes of pink. Already, I was planning.

"I could use the sash for the valance and piece the two fronts together for one curtain, and the back for another. Do you think Mrs. Ajarian would let us paint? We could do the walls in soft blue and the dresser in medium blue for contrast, and we'd have the prettiest bedroom in town."

He agreed wholeheartedly. "Sure. Then *House and Garden* will want to photograph it, and they'll pay us five thousand dollars for the privileges and we can loaf the rest of our lives."

"Oh, Bruce!" I laughed, pulling him onto the bed beside me. "What would I do without you?"

He smiled a little ruefully. "You wouldn't be sitting in this ugly barn trying to make a home out of a hole."

"I'd rather be with you in this hole than with anyone else anywhere else." I snuggled against him a moment, then asked, "But, Bruce, you haven't said a word about this morning. What did you find out?"

51

"I register Friday. Classes start next Tuesday. And my student grant will come through. It's not much — if my grades had been higher through the first three years, I could have received more, but it will help."

"What student grant? I didn't know you'd applied for any. Why didn't you tell me?"

"I didn't want you disappointed, in case I didn't get it." He rose, stretched, and took off his ridiculous Arabian robe, not for a moment realizing he'd thrown a damper on our joy. I wanted him to confide, to share things, that we might pray matters through together, but for the time being, this was not his habit. Perhaps it never would be.

Mrs. Ajarian would not give permission to repaint her walls. She said they had been done a year ago, and she could not afford to cater to every tenant's whim. After that, I hardly dared bring up the subject of paint for the dresser. I bought a small can of blue enamel for sixty-nine cents, and painted it myself. In a second hand store we found a cheap pink lampshade, which we used to soften the glare in the bedroom. The curtains, all sewed by hand, proved a headache. Arabian robes are not cut like straight drapes. I was forced to make them narrower than I'd planned, and piece where I had not planned. The material was slippery to handle. After hours of labor and frustration, they were finished and hung. We closed the bedroom door, opened it again, switched on the light, and pretended astonishment at the transformation.

By this time, I was tired of miracle-working. The kitchen needed attention, but it did not lend itself easily to remodeling. We decided to let it wait. We never did get any bright ideas on the subject.

Our tenement house was very narrow. Across the hall from us dwelt a solitary creature, silent by day, making only occasional noises by night. Directly above us lived an elderly couple, too grumpy even to smile when we met in the hall. Twice I saw a young girl dash furtively up the stairs, her thin legs flashing in an air of desperation. I wanted to speak to her, to let her know I was harmless, but she could not be approached.

Seven souls under one roof, all going our own way, not speaking, not caring. It was very strange.

Bruce left for registration on Friday. I had put off a dread task as long as my conscience allowed. That day I had to go job-hunting. Perhaps with that same idea of sparing Bruce undue concern, I did not tell him of my plans. I, too, prayed alone. Then I showered and dressed very carefully, selecting my trimmest suit and neatest hat. I could not afford to look young, but I knew of no instant aging process. I did the best I could with what I had.

Mrs. Ajarian, as grudgingly as if it cost her money, gave me directions to the central office of education. I could have driven the car, but the prospect of city driving made me nervous. Public transportation was more convenient.

As the bus jolted through the mid-morning traffic, the very indifference of those about me began to affect me. My stomach crawled with nervous tension. We had very little money. Suppose I didn't get a job?

But, of course, I would get a job! Were not teachers in short supply all through the country? I knew the Lord had promised to go with me and undertake for all our needs.

Alternating between outright fear and mild trepidation, I completed the trip to the education office. It occupied one wing of West End High School, a forbidding-looking brick building surrounded by black asphalt. The imaginative city planners had named Sheldon's three high schools West End, East End, and North End. Some day, there would be a South End. And then, what would they do for names? Better not to let the city expand any farther.

A pleasant, middle-aged secretary took my name, looked over my credentials, and disappeared into an inner office. In a minute or two, she returned with a smile.

"Mr. Townsend is busy on the phone. He'll talk to you in a few moments."

The first hurdle was over. I sat back with a sigh of relief. My fingers were ice cold, and trembling as if from a near-mishap. I tried not to fidget. Then the secretary was smiling, standing at her desk.

"Mr. Townsend is free now, Mrs. King. Please follow me."

I entered his office, my mind almost in neutral. Mr. Townsend was a short man, very slight in build, with a clipped mustache over a small mouth. Wrinkles etched his face, but they struck me instantly as having been acquired more from the cares of getting ahead in the world than from any great depth of character. His manner, brusquely courteous, was a forewarning of the interview. He stood up and offered me a soft, clammy hand with a smile to match. I peered into light, colorless eyes which told me immediately all I wanted to know.

He looked over my transcripts and teachers' certificate, obviously not impressed.

"Well, Mrs. King," he said finally, forming a tent with the

tips of his fingers, "if you were qualified to teach kindergarten, or first grade, we might find a place for you. But — don't you think you're a bit young to tackle junior high youngsters? After all, this is a most critical period in their lives."

"I've taught that age group one semester, Mr. Townsend," I pointed out.

"But in a private *academy,* Mrs. King! And a *religious* one, at that! I'm very sorry. If you care to leave your name, and phone number, perhaps we could use you for a substitute teacher from time to time."

He held out my folder. I took it, saying, "Mr. Townsend, I have to put my husband through medical school. I must have regular, assured income."

"I see," he said. He held the door for me, closing it the moment I stepped into the hall.

I hadn't exactly expected heralds and fanfare, but I thought my reception in the superintendent's office very shabby. Those articles about the teacher shortage certainly hadn't been read in Sheldon! All the years of grinding study, only to be told I really didn't meet with Mr. Townsend's concept of a junior high teacher. He was the school superintendent. There was no other appeal. After the deflation, I would not have had courage for one, anyway. I seethed with resentment. I had been completely unprepared for a failure, or for another course of action. Teaching was the only thing I could do well.

In the planning stage, life seems simple. We plan to do this and that, and then this and that, with no allowances for interruptions or obstacles, certainly no room for failure or frustration! How different the real thing is!

In the schoolyard, implanted in the black asphalt, was a green wooden bench facing on the street. I sat down to quiet my trembling knees and to collect my disarranged thoughts. A seedy looking character in a brown tweed coat two sizes too big for him, ambled by, then turned and sat on the other end of my bench. Gradually he edged closer. I got up and left.

And then the pangs of hunger reminded me, that, job or not, I still needed to eat. I couldn't bear to return to our empty apartment to brood over my morning. Bruce would not be in until late afternoon. Out on the street, midst the bustle of busy people all going somewhere, doing something, my disappointment seemed less intense.

Down a side street, stuffed into a row of uninteresting business offices, like a squeezed marshmallow, stood a bright white and black sandwich shop. "Sam's," it said simply. I slipped in, ordered a tuna-fish-on-wheat and a glass of milk.

The waiter (I assumed he was Sam) moved with the easy dexterity of one long accustomed to the motions. The place was small, and only one other customer sat at the counter. When I could, I attracted his attention.

"Would you happen to need help?" I asked, not really caring, but making a stab in the dark.

Sam shrugged, and ran a hand through his salt and pepper hair. "Naw. My wife does the cooking, and I take care of this end of the business. If we hire a girl, we gotta bother with Social Security, withholding tax, state tax — too much red tape. We stay small, this way, but we make a living without ulcers."

He leaned against the cash register. "Why? You lookin' for a job? Whyn'cha apply in one of these business offices?"

"I don't know shorthand and I don't like secretarial work. I've had lots of experience as a waitress."

"Yeah?" Sam grinned. "You don't look as if you've had lots of experience at anything. Look, Sis, if you want a job, don't come in a little joint like this. I take one look at you, I know you'd quit after the first pay check. You go to a place with class— the Neuchatelle or Alphand's" (he pronounced it New *Chat*tel or *Al*fand's) "any of them French-sounding restaurants, and you stand a better chance."

The lone customer at the far end of the counter got to his feet and cleared his throat. Sam left to take his money. I had finished my sandwich. There seemed no point in hanging around. I put the exact change beside my plate, waved a hand at Sam, and departed, feeling much better. Mr. Townsend had not cared for me, but Sam had implied I had "class."

After three days of ugly, threatening weather, Sunday smiled at us with a promise of spring surely being not "far behind." A streak of light gold streaming in through our east window lightened up the gray of our living quarters. We relaxed through a leisurely breakfast of pancakes and sausages, forgetting the tensions of the past week. Four hundred and twelve Prospect Street was beginning to feel like home.

It was odd that, after all these months, it was in the house of God that I should feel my first painful twinges of homesickness. Trentwood Memorial Church, where Bruce held his membership, occupied an entire city block in the midst of a well-to-do neighborhood. Tall oaks and maples stretched their unleafed branches in a surrealistic arch above the street. The yellow brick building lacked the simple grace of our New England churches. Here all was functional, nothing wasted on mere beauty. The windows were plain rectangles, the doors a dark brown. It could have been a school, or a courthouse, or just about anything. It happened to be a church.

The interior, however, was lovely. Light natural wood walls and pews, thick beige-and-brown carpeting gave an impression of quiet elegance. A tall, slender cross mounted on the wall behind the pulpit reminded the worshiper at once of the Risen Christ. Accustomed as I was to white pews and maroon draperies, in my mind I was forced to concede the superiority of this atmosphere. Soft organ music filled the church, and people took their places quickly for quiet prayer before the service. No friendly smiles exchanged, no cordial handshakes, only serious faces turned toward the platform.

In this church Bruce had received most of his spiritual training. Prior to adulthood, his only acquaintance with church had been at Christmas and Easter. When he had at last been introduced to the joys of Christianity, he had formed an impression of Trentwood as being the Model Church.

Not so with me. In New England, except for a few community churches, denominationalism is strong. I would have preferred a smaller church of my own denomination, where the people were friendly, and opportunities for service more abundant. In a church as large as this, it was obvious only professionally trained members would be asked to work. The choir was excellent, the organist nearly perfect. Ushers, with white carnations in their dark blue suits, moved along the aisles as smoothly as at a well-rehearsed wedding. Nothing of the novice was evident here.

I longed for my own church, where every newcomer was recognized and made welcome, where everyone found a place to fill. Most of all, I wanted to find our friends and activities centered in our church home, for surely they would not be with Bruce's fellow students or my fellow workers.

But not even my critical ear could find fault with the message or the messenger. Dear Doctor McPherson was as close to a true apostle as I had ever found. His whole being emanated Love. Off his tongue with the faint Scotch brogue rolled some of the most eloquent oratory I had ever heard. He was not lofty, as some learned men are, but on every man's level. In the truest sense of the word, Dr. McPherson was a "minister."

At the close of the service, official "greeters" stood in the lobby to assist the pastor with hand-shaking. Feeling as wooden-faced as the rest of the congregation looked, I would have passed on out to the street. But a high-pitched voice chirped, "Oh, hi, there! You're back! Are you going to stay?"

I looked down at a tiny little wren of a girl about my own age. Her feet and hands were those of a child's. But she was dressed like a young woman, and her face revealed considerable maturity.

"You don't remember me, do you?" she continued in a rapid flow. "I'm Betty Thurston. You sat beside me at the young adults party we had one night at the pastor's last spring. Remember?"

"Oh, of course!" I smiled, warm for the first time that hour. Betty had been great fun, but I had completely forgotten her existence.

"And this is my husband, Bob." She indicated a gawky young man beside her. He said nothing, but smiled. Betty went on, "Are you married now? I've forgotten your name, but I know this is Bruce King."

"Yes. We were married last June. My name is Sandy."

"Glad you're back, Sandy and Bruce. Don't forget — young adults meet tonight at 5:45. Do come. We need you."

Need? In this church? But it was good to be welcomed so cordially. My entire feeling performed a complete turnabout.

Dr. McPherson was a very busy pastor. His people almost had to make an appointment to say "hello" to him. But, somehow, he always had time for Bruce.

"Come over after church tonight for cake and coffee," he invited, without consulting his wife.

So we, and the Thurstons, and two other young couples spent a happy hour in the McPherson home that evening.

It required no great insight to comprehend Bruce's complete trust in the McPhersons as spiritual counselors. Usually, I spurn this type of idealization, for I have lived with Christians most of my life. I know the folly of enshrouding even the best of them with virtues seldom attained before Heaven. But the McPhersons *were* different. Even in their physical presence there was beauty.

America is said to worship Youth. Why, I do not know. For youth is composed of uncertainty and stumbling, erring judgments and bitter mistakes. To grow old as the McPhersons were doing — gracefully, serenely, calm in the face of the Lord's will — this was genuine beauty.

Dr. McPherson was a big man, nearly six feet four. His skin was clear and pink as a baby's. Bushy white brows topped piercing ice-blue eyes. Tiny laugh wrinkles creased his eyes and mouth. Despite frequent applications of hair tonic, his white thatch of hair was thick and unruly. With a bright red suit, he would have presented the perfect pose of Père Noel.

He had earned his doctor's degree in philosophy, then left a promising academic career to become a humble minister of God. Though his sermons were thickly larded with evidence of his wide background of knowledge, he preached directly and only from the Word. He was completely in love with Jesus Christ.

Mrs. McPherson, several years his junior, possessed that rare commodity known as common sense. She acted as ballast to her heavenly-soaring husband. She checked his Bible to be certain his notes were within: she reminded him to put on his coat before facing the wintry blast. Their love was evident — tender, certain, humorous. Unashamed, he leaned on her for all practical details of life.

Along the couch, my hand reached for Bruce's. No lover of sentimentality, he could not have known my thoughts. But he looked away from the McPhersons and smiled into my eyes.

CHAPTER FIVE

Inconsistency plagues the most consistent. Though I desperately wanted Bruce to share everything with me, I found there were things I could not share with him. When, the Friday before, I had returned from job-hunting, my disappointment had been so sickening, I had not even wanted to discuss it. Triumphs are much easier to share than defeats. Bruce, lacking the vaguest knowledge of what women do to fill their hours at home, had not even realized I had been out that morning.

For two days, in surreptitious secrecy, I had combed the Help Wanted ads, praying the Lord would lead me to the right job. Nearly a full column of Help Wanted: Female ads listed such desirable employees as:

General Housekeeper: Live In
Licensed Practical Nurse
Experienced Stitchers
Hairdresser
Salesgirls
Stenographers

None of these occupations seemed to fit my limited talents. After much wrestling inwardly, I decided to take my friend Sam's advice and apply at one of "them French-sounding restaurants."

For no other reason than that it was closest to the bus stop, I entered Alphand's. The shaking knees, the crawling stomach were still there, but better disguised this time.

The manager came striding from the back of the restaurant so rapidly I feared he would run me over. I stepped aside and he stopped abruptly. If he drove the way he walked, I wondered how many rear collisions he caused each week. But he was much easier to talk to than Mr. Townsend had been.

"Where'd you work before?" he asked, when I told him I had had three years' experience as a waitress.

"At the Grey Briars on Cape Cod for three summers. Four winters at Harbrook College."

"Grey Briars?" He repeated with a quizzical lift of his bushy eyebrows. "Did you know Jake Hollister?"

"Yes. He was the head waiter my first two summers there."

"Okay. You're hired." He dropped his employer manner-isms and held out his hand. "My name's Ken Mylan. Am I glad to see you, girl. I just lost a waitress this morning. If you'd applied a day earlier, I'd have turned you down."

It was another small working of the Lord. He knew how bruising an experience I'd had a few days before with the super-intendent, and He'd kept me from applying for this job when it was not open.

Mr. Mylan led the way to the kitchen, where he introduced the maître d'hotel and two waitresses, the cook and the salad girl. At that hour, there were few diners, and we had time to talk a bit.

With a thin, sallow face, a pinched-looking nose, and quick-darting black eyes, the maître d' resembled nothing more than a fox. I wondered how we would get along. He was also a pincher and a patter. With my first paycheck, I vowed I would purchase a steel corset.

Some people count sheep — others put themselves to sleep thinking up new rules for other people to obey. The maître d' was one of these. (We never called him by his name — he was always the maître d'.) In a needlessly authoritative voice, he listed his private rules for the dining room. No speaking to patrons except on business. No talking in the kitchen except on business. No wearing of jewelry. No flat shoes.

The uniforms were black nylon, with frilled white aprons and perky white caps, all in keeping with the "French atmosphere." Outside of a few French foods on the menu, however, the restaurant was thoroughly American. The owner's real name was Albert, but "Albert's" was not nearly as high-class as "Alphand's." What's in a name? Several thousand dollars.

My hours were to be seven to three, with a ten-minute coffee break when I could take it. This, again was an answer to unuttered prayer, for now Bruce and I could have our evenings together. With spring on its way, early rising would present no problem.

The work was second nature to me, much less of a strain than teaching would have been. My customers were well-to-do businessmen who ignored me completely except for very decent tipping. The prospects looked good.

Bruce was in the apartment when I arrived. "Where've you been? Job-hunting?" he asked.

"No — working. I am now a waitress at Alphand's."

"Waitress? I thought you were going to teach!"

"I thought so, too, but the school department had other ideas. They could only offer me substitute teaching, and then we'd have to install a telephone, and Bruce, we need more money than that!"

"Oh, but Sandy, I never wanted to let my wife do such — such hard work." (He said "hard," but he meant "menial." There was still a bit of the snob left in Bruce.) Then he thought of something else.

"That's only a few blocks from Uncle Larry's store. Suppose he comes in for lunch some day?"

"Suppose he does?"

"Nothing, I suppose, but it would only make him more smug."

"What do we care? We said we'd live our own life, and we will! All he has left is his money. Let him add smugness to it if he wants."

"Oh, Sandy!" Bruce, wavering between exasperation and surrender, finally surrendered.

Our lives settled quickly into a routine. We rose at six each morning, ate breakfast, and I departed for work, leaving Bruce free to study till his eight or nine o'clock classes. Arriving home at three-thirty in the afternoon, I had time to tidy the apartment and start supper before Bruce arrived from campus. He found it less distracting to study in the library there than in the apartment where I was prone to bang brooms and dustpans around.

When he appeared home a full hour early one evening, I looked up from my first attempt at *beef Stroganoff*.

"Sandy, there's a man interested in buying our car," he announced.

"Our car? Are we selling it?"

"Well, it costs four fifty a week just to keep it in the lot. Gas costs money, and with the bus as close as it is, we don't really *need* a car."

A gift from his uncle when Bruce had been discharged from the veteran's hospital, the car had been an expensive model. It was in excellent condition, with hardly a speck of rust on its body.

"I suppose it would be the practical thing to do," I admitted. "But, Bruce, do you really want to give it up? You love that car."

He smiled crookedly and looked away. "I've given up a few other things I love. And I don't miss them."

Not much you don't, I thought. Aloud, I said, "Let's pray about it. How much is he offering you?"

"Five hundred. It would be enough to pay off the rest of the semester's tuition."

We sold the car, Bruce's last link to his past life of luxury. Then, to appease the wrench, we went out to the only steak dinner in our married life.

He stood in the hall one afternoon, his hand poised to knock, when I suddenly pulled the door open, about to run out to mail a letter.

"Excuse me, ma'am, could I borrow a little coffee? I'm all out and . . . ." he shrugged, not finishing the sentence.

He was the queerest specimen of adult man I had ever seen — rather like an elderly teen-ager. Under a plaid sport shirt flecked with grease and coffee stains, he wore a black turtle-neck sweater. Faded blue jeans and ragged, dirty white sneakers completed the ensemble. His black hair had not been cut for two or three months, and not combed for as many days. He had shaved, but it served him no good purpose, for his face and neck were covered with severe case of acne. A large nose and prominent yellow teeth almost obscured his one really good feature — luminous black eyes fringed with curling eyelashes so long they appeared artificial.

61

Very slight of frame, his eye-level was only an inch or two above mine.

I sucked in my breath with surprise, and managed a calm reply. "I only have regular grind. My husband doesn't like instant coffee."

I stepped back into our apartment to find the coffee for him. Distressingly, he followed me inside. And then I didn't know how to get rid of him.

"My name is Adelbert Coogan," he announced. (Accent on the second syllable. I had always wondered how to pronounce that name!)

He seemed to be waiting expectantly. I was about to introduce myself, when he went on, "Ah, I see the name means nothing to you. You don't read *Poetry Review?*"

"Not recently," I answered, feeling apologetic, for no known reason. I had never heard of *Poetry Review*.

"My work was the central discussion point last month," he reported modestly. This was not terribly surprising. We lived in a university town. Almost anything was likely to turn up.

"Oh? What kind of poetry do you write?"

"I deal with complexities of life from an existential viewpoint."

I handed him some coffee in a small jar. He took it and continued to stand, first on one foot, then the other. He was waiting for an invitation to sit down. But my New England reserve questioned the propriety of entertaining a strange man with my husband out of the house.

"Have you published a great deal?" I inquired, not really wanting to know.

"No. I polish my work until its words gleam with truth and beauty before I submit it to the cruel eyes of an editor. Do you know what murder these editors commit? They pull a work to shreds, till the very essence is lost in the mists of obscurity."

Such a winged flight of oratory demanded something more than the mundane "That's too bad," I murmured, only because I could think of nothing else to say. I needn't have worried. He never listened to responses. He only craved a sounding board.

"I live across the hall. Would you like to hear some of my latest efforts?"

I should have been ashamed to throw a damper on this enthusiasm. But it was getting late, and Bruce would be home at five.

"Sometime," I said, again feeling apologetic. It was a bit

like thrusting a wiggling, eager pup out into the cold. "I have to mail this letter, and then get supper for my husband."

I walked toward the door and he had no choice but to take a few steps backward to find himself once more in the hall.

Some people have sensibilities wrapped in asbestos. He returned the following afternoon, this time with a sheaf of papers half an inch thick. Apparently, he considered a second meeting a friendship of long standing, for he no longer waited for an invitation. He took a chair at the table and began to read his poetry in a spell-binding, sonorous voice. His entire demeanor changed. His eyes flashed, his fists clenched, his voice rolled in a rumble of low thunder. His verse dealt with the cheerful subjects of desolation, disillusionment, and disfigurement and rape.

He was familiar with the existential thought of the day, from Camus to Sartre. One poem ran something like this:

"The man on the cross still hangs,
    In useless agony.
    His vision gone,
    By God forsaken,
    His 'why?' echoes on in the gloom."

I felt uneasy, helpless, on the defensive. Why did these non-believers always return to the one subject they could not fathom? They pictured Jesus abandoned, betrayed, deceived, misunderstood — but never could they catch the faintest glimmer of a Risen Saviour sent to redeem mankind. He haunted them. In turn, they sought to trample what they could not comprehend — the faith of the simple in mind. They agonized, they whined, they pondered in depth, and still the mystery persisted. Perhaps Calvin was right — this glorious salvation was only for the elect. Surely communication with followers of such philosophy seemed destined for failure.

There was another verse, from a longer poem called *The Pit*. Here my neighbor depicted all humanity as a mass of struggling worms, caught in the mire of life, unable to remove themselves. The final verse concluded in limerick form,

"The slimy black of the murky depths
    Cries out in anguished pain
    There is no god
    There is no soul
    There is only the curse of Cain."

It wasn't particularly original verse, but his outlook distressed me more than his lack of talent.

"Is that what you really think? Or are you just trying to set a mood?"

Adelbert Coogan was offended. He answered stiltedly, "Of course it's what I think. Existence holds no joys — only degrees of sorrow."

"But we have more than *existence* — we have *life!* And life is a God-given privilege!"

"That's what they tell in Sunday school to pacify the populace."

"Perhaps if you did your writing in the daytime and slept at night, you'd have a different perspective," I retorted.

"Why should I? We live in a nightmare. People feed on people." He sounded like a parrot, repeating someone else's philosophy. Surely he was too young to have experienced such morbid emptiness himself.

"Then you don't associate with the right kind. People have faults, but they aren't essentially evil."

He fluttered his cow-like eyelashes in a gesture of helplessness. Then, to change the subject, he rose and ambled over to the wavery mirror hanging over my sink, where he studiously scrutinized his face from every available angle, pausing now and again to squeeze a pimple.

"Mrs. King," he observed, more unruffled than I, "you think like a peasant."

"I do," I agreed. "I'd rather be a peasant than a poet. We're much happier. And I might add, healthier."

"If ignorance is bliss, you ought to be."

"What makes you think it's so intelligent to see nothing but slime and muck? It's like eating out of the garbage pail when good food lies on the table."

"Ah, but it's Truth. Was it Shelley — no, Keats, who so wisely said, 'Beauty is Truth, Truth Beauty'? And Beauty lies in the eyes of the beholder."

"I don't know what you're talking about. I wonder if you do."

Our voices had been so loud, neither of us had heard Bruce's footsteps on the stairway, though he was no lightweight. He appeared in the open doorway, an incredulous look in his eyes.

"What's going on here? I thought someone was having a fight."

I laughed. Adelbert did not. He scrambled to his feet, hastily assembling his papers. Beside him, Bruce looked like a giant. Neither of the men greeted one another with any warmth, though I introduced them naturally enough. With the inherent suspicion the man of science feels for the man of letters, Bruce exchanged only the stiffest of amenities with our neighbor. Mr. Coogan did not linger. Bruce closed the door firmly behind him and turned to me.

"How'd he get in here?" he demanded.

My gorge rose. I opened my innocent brown eyes wide. "He walked in. Why?"

"Do you mean you let a strange man into our apartment when you were alone?"

"That little thing? What do you think he could do to me?" I pulled a frying pan from the cupboard and set it on the stove.

"Sandy, you're not stupid! Stop being naive! You can't trust every stranger who comes along."

"You sound like a stuffed shirt. Anyone who writes poetry as pitiful as his would be completely harmless."

"I don't care what kind of poetry he writes, I don't want him hanging around here any more!"

Were we having the first quarrel of our married life over Adelbert Coogan? I burst out laughing. "Oh, Bruce, don't tell me you're jealous!"

He grinned. "No, I'm not jealous. I just don't like him."

"How do you know? All you did was glare at him a minute or two. If you ever looked at me like that, I'd wither and die."

He caught me in his arms. "Please don't wither up and die. Maybe I'm over-cautious. But, Sandy, don't let anything happen to you, please."

"Once you told me only the good die young. Have you changed your mind, or have I suddenly become good?"

"You're the goodest thing that ever happened to me." He kissed the top of my head, and abruptly released me.

"What's for dinner? I didn't have time for lunch today."

Which explained his unwonted crankiness. I made a mental note never to tease a hungry man.

I expected to see no more of Adelbert Coogan. For a couple of days my thoughts were occupied with responses I should have made. I should have told him this, or explained that to him, for he had no clear picture of true Christianity. In the heat of argument, I had failed to remain calm and get down to the bare essentials. Failure always stung.

It was the same at work. I never could anticipate the questions so I would have a good answer. When I announced that

65

Bruce and I planned to be missionaries, I might as well have stated that we had taken up sword swallowing as a sideline.

"What for?" asked the maître d'. "Aren't there enough heathen in this country? What business do you have, telling other people how to live?"

"We're not going for that purpose. We're going to tell them Jesus saves from sin."

"Oh, yeah?" And he walked out of the kitchen in huge disgust. It was the end of that discussion. But it served a useful purpose. Without benefit of steel corset, Mr. Pinch and Pat stayed away from me.

CHAPTER SIX

The only thing which distinguished our neighborhood from a slum was the lack of trash lying about its streets. No trees, no lawns, not even a window box, gave evidence of nature's loveliness. The tenement buildings, cemented together like Siamese quadruplets, ran on for block after dingy block, covered with a pall of mill soot. Children, perpetually dirty, played hopscotch or kick-the-can on the sidewalks. Their elders bustled in and out of the many small businesses on the ground floor — the barber shop, the automatic laundry, the cut-rate milk store, and Mrs. Ajarian's corner store. Fortunately, the taverns were all on other blocks. Twice I had to step over a man, dead drunk, sprawled in the entrance way to our apartment. He was Mr. Davenport, from the apartment directly over ours, and perfectly harmless, Mrs. Ajarian assured me.

It seems ridiculous to have enjoyed living in a dump like that. But we did! Faces became familiar, a few tentative smiles were exchanged, the walk between our apartment and the bus stop became home territory. When a trucker called out for directions to a certain street and I was able to give them, I knew Sheldon was my home!

One afternoon as I returned from work, I saw a pale cream convertible pulled up to the curb in front of our doorway. As I came even with it, Pat King opened the door and called,

"Sandy!" Her husky voice, half eager, half reproachful, sounded almost too refined in surroundings such as these.

"Pat!" We embraced. Pat always smelled of boudoir fragrance, her perfume expensively subtle.

"Why didn't you call?" she asked. "How long have you been in Sheldon?"

"Nearly three weeks. How did you find us?"

"I knew the second semester had begun. I called the University office and they gave me Bruce's address. But why didn't you call?"

I hedged. It seemed quite tactless to say we had forgotten. This section of Sheldon was so different from her area that there was nothing to remind me of that other side of town. Pat and Don had made no effort to keep in touch with us since the wedding — not even a card at Christmas. With everything new to occupy my thoughts, I had pushed thoughts of Bruce's family to the back of my mind. His uncle, of course, was out of the question, but the estrangement with Don and Pat had never been complete. Bruce should have made some contact.

"I'm sorry, Pat, but I wanted to get settled before inviting you over. Look, you're going to get a parking ticket if you leave the car here. I'll ride down to the lot with you, then we can walk back together."

Pat had no boots on her beautifully clad feet, and the walk beneath us was sloppy with old slush. By the time we reached our apartment, her shoes were thoroughly soaked, and I felt like a neglectful mother. Silently she followed me up the dark stairway with its old-building smell. I unlocked the door and led her inside. She stood in the entrance, her eyes wide with shock.

"Oh, Sandy! Is this where you live?"

For an instant, I fought back resentment. This was my home — I considered it a very pleasant place. The floor was newly waxed, the curtains freshly starched, and the wall lamp cast a softening glow on the wall. But Pat had spent her life in luxury. She could spend a hundred and twenty-five dollars on a street dress. To her, our quarters were nothing less than a hovel.

"It's very comfortable," I assured her. "We have plenty of hot water, and really, Pat, we spend very little time here. Bruce goes to classes, and I go to work all day."

"Oh? What kind of work? Are you teaching?"

"No. I'm waiting tables at Alphand's."

"Alphand's! My women's club goes there for lunch every month!" She was so horror-stricken that I laughed out loud.

"Let me know in advance, Pat, and I'll put a big black mustache on. No one will ever guess who I am."

"Oh, they won't remember you, anyway," she assured herself, completely unconscious of her snobbery.

I set the coffee cups on the table and fixed the electric percolator. Thank the Lord for wedding gifts! At least my table service was good.

Pat took a turn about the apartment, glancing into our bedroom and bathroom. In her purple stretch slacks, she looked even taller and more perfectly formed than I had remembered. She was a truly beautiful girl, with not a malicious bone in her body.

"Sandy," she asked thoughtfully, as she returned to the living room, "how much are you paying for this place?"

"Sixty dollars a month."

"You could find something in a nicer neighborhood for a hundred. I'd give you the extra forty out of my clothing allowance. Don would never know."

Poor girl meant well. I must be careful not to let my irritation show. "Thanks, Pat," I said, trying to sound sincere. "But you know how Bruce is. Don't mention it to him. He'd think you were offering charity."

"But I'm not! I think it's terrible the way Uncle Larry is holding Bruce's money from him! He has every right to it!"

"We're doing better without it," I said. "How is Uncle Larry?"

A shadow crossed her violet eyes. "I don't see him much. Don still works for him, of course. But we don't go over to the big house often, and he doesn't come to see us. The Kings aren't like the Marshalls, you know. That's why I've missed you so. I haven't anyone close."

In spite of her height, Pat always aroused the maternal instinct in me. I wanted to pat her on the shoulder, or pull her close, tell her everything would be all right.

"Is your mother still in California?" I asked.

Pat's hand shook. "I think so. She left her husband. Or maybe he left her. She's studying astrology now. She wrote me a while ago to tell me Don and I were not suited for each other, because our birthdays are too close. Don was mad and told me not to answer."

"Did you?"

"No. I'm not much of a letter-writer. I tried to call several times, but she was never home, and it seemed too much trouble."

"But, Pat, she's your mother. You don't have to talk about astrology, but you ought to let her know you love her."

Pat shrugged, her violet eyes brimming. "I don't. I never have. You don't know what it's like — having a mother you can't talk to!"

No, I didn't. And I suppose I never would appreciate completely what my family meant to me.

"Pat, if you loved the Lord, I think you'd love your mother."

She sighed, her shoulders hunched together in dejection. "I wish I could. I went to church twice, but it's lonely by myself. Don won't go near a church. He says religion divides instead of unites. It's pulled Bruce away from his family, and caused a lot of trouble with my mother."

"But your mother isn't stable. She's dabbled in so many religions she doesn't know which side is up."

"I know. But try to tell Don that."

I poured her a second cup of coffee. "Pat, you know you need the Lord," I said.

"How could I be sure I'd found Him? There are too many religions. You and Bruce — you seem so happy and confident — but tell me, Sandy, do you ever doubt?"

"I used to. But that was before——" my voice trailed off, thinking back.

"Before I met the Lord. Pat, when you were a little girl, did you ever wonder how you would know when you were really in love?"

"Yes."

"But when you met Don, did you doubt your love for him?"

She smiled. "I've always loved Don. More than he loves me."

"But you had lots of other boy friends."

"Yes, but they weren't important. I never loved any of them but Don."

"How did you *know?*"

"It was just *right* when we were together, that's all. The way he smiled, and looked at me——" She broke off. "I thought we were talking about the Lord."

"We are. That's how it is when you meet the Lord. Somehow, it all seems right. Deep down, you know it's true — He is your Saviour. But you have to make the first step of faith."

Those marvelous lavender eyes, unconscious of their beauty, spilled over. "How? Sandy, tell me, how?"

"Believe His Word, Pat. Jesus came to earth to die for your sins. He took your guilt on Himself so that you could become a child of God. Ask Him to forgive your sins, then believe He has done it."

"It's too simple. Don't I have to *do* something?"

"No. What kind of gift is it if you earn it? 'For by grace are ye saved by faith, not of works, lest any man should boast.'"

Like a swimmer taking his first dive, Pat took a deep breath. "I'll try."

She bowed her head, and her lips moved, but she did not pray aloud. When the silence grew long enough to be uncomfortable, I prayed for her, pleading with the Lord to open Pat's understanding, to the beauty of Christ's simple Gospel. When I had finished, I looked up. Pat was staring at the checked tablecloth.

"Are you satisfied, Pat?" I asked in a low voice. "Or would you like me to continue praying?"

"No. I thought — I expected to *feel* something. You said when you became a Christian, all the world seemed to glow with joy. Nothing glows for me. Do you think it ever will?"

Every person's salvation experience is different. My own had been as Pat remembered — glowing and joyful. My best friend, Phyl's, had been highly emotional, the end of a long struggle. Perhaps Pat's would be a gradual one, for her spiritual knowledge was scant. Like any new baby, she needed growth before she achieved enlightenment.

"Meet us at the Trentwood Church, Sunday," I urged. "We'll sit together, and perhaps you'll become more assured of salvation as time goes on."

"All right. Don sleeps late Sunday mornings. He won't care if I don't disturb him."

Bruce came in, as she was preparing to leave. The sight of her pale face shocked him, but he recovered quickly. He wanted her to stay, so he could visit with her, but it was growing late. The King men expected their women to be home when they arrived from work.

"I'll see you Sunday," Pat promised.

Only after she had gone did I realize that she had not invited us to their home.

Slowly it began to dawn on me exactly how sheltered my life had been. When Bruce first became interested in me, he often wore a puzzled expression. Once he said, "You really think 'God's in His Heaven, All's right with the world,' don't you?"

His implication that I was naive had offended me, for at the time I considered myself quite a lady of the world. After all, I had been away from home for nearly three years, had quite neatly severed the strings which bound me to Bartlett as the center of the world's importance. Almost everyone I had ever known, however, was pleasant, respectable, quasi-religious; not given to any open dishonesty or scandal. Dope addiction, perversion, were only words to me — certainly not within the experience of necessity.

Here, in our Prospect Street apartment, the rosy-tinted glasses gradually cleared. People touched on the fringe of our lives, so different from any I had ever known, that I began to realize that Bruce and I were abnormal in our normality. Sometimes, like actors in a poorly-organized play, they strutted across the stage, mouthed their lines, and bowed out, never to be heard from again. Other times, they became an integral part of our current lives.

Bruce, who had never been an adherent to the "All's right with the world" philosophy, suffered no disillusionment. In subtle ways, though, he changed. From a stand-offish, touch-me-not attitude, he became a sympathetic listener. Unlike me, he could adopt an objective viewpoint. He was concerned, but he was not *involved,* thus sparing himself many sleepless hours.

For over a week, we had seen nothing of our poetic neighbor. Then, one afternoon, just as I pulled out a basket of ironing, he returned, this time towing a young girl behind him.

"She's our chaperon," he said to me, with a jerk of his shaggy head in the girl's direction. "I wouldn't want that big brute to come in here again and find me with you — brrr!" he shivered in mock fear.

He turned to the dark-haired girl. "Tam, this is — uh — now, I've forgotten——"

The door still stood open. Adelbert caught his hands on either side of the doorway, leaned back into the hallway, read our name card on the door and continued, "Mrs. King!"

He was a Maynard G. Krebs with intellect. His looselimbed motions made everything about him comical. If he had chosen the stage rather than poetry for his career, he would have been an overnight sensation.

Now he waved a grandiloquent hand toward the couch, and the girl sat down. She caught my interest, for she was slender to the point of fragility. Dark wavy hair formed a curtain about her face, almost obscuring her soulful black eyes. Within her seemed buried all the sorrows known to woman. I knew who she was, of course, the frightened girl from the floor above.

Adelbert was talking, but I ignored him.

"I'm sorry," I said to her, "I didn't hear your name."

"Tamara," she responded briefly, a surname being apparently superfluous.

"That's pretty," I said, and could have kicked myself for sounding condescending. "Mine is Sandy."

She did not consider this information worthy of acknowledgment, for she looked down and picked at the pleat in her plaid skirt. She appeared no older than a high school girl. I could not imagine why she lived alone in this dreary tenement. An "affair" between her and Adelbert struck me as highly unlikely, for there was no exchange of glances, no tender brushing of the hands. Adelbert accorded Tamara no more attention than my kitchen lamp.

He had brought with him the inevitable sheaf of poetry, for he had failed to distinguish between a *devotée* and a polite listener. Or perhaps he felt that to know his work was to love it. For the next fifteen minutes, while I ironed, and Tamara stared blankly at the wall, Adelbert treated us to the rolling of his sonorous voice as he dramatized the efforts of the last two weeks' writing. At the end, he looked up with a puppy dog grin.

"It takes longer to write this stuff than to read it," he said.

I laughed. "Why don't you take up acting? You're very good, you know."

"You mean, a good poet, or a good actor?" I'm certain my opinion meant nothing to him — he wanted only an admiring echo chamber.

"Your verse is too morbid. You don't really feel that way, you're just aping the current thought of the day."

He waved his hand in the air in a gesture of disgust. "You Pollyannas make me sick!" he cried.

But his anger was not genuine. He liked to take an unpopular stance just to watch the reaction. Having grown up with brothers and boy cousins, I could not take him too seriously.

"Let's ask Tam," I suggested, to draw her into the conversation. "What do you think of Adelbert's writing?"

"I don't know. I wasn't listening," she replied disinterestedly. She was the most passive person I had ever met.

"How could you help it? He was practically yelling."

"Easy," offered Adelbert. "She detaches herself from the

world around her. It's the only way she stays sane. There are times when I'm not sure she *is* sane."

He discussed her as if she were not there. I turned to her again. "What do you do all day, Tam? Work? Or are you still in school?"

"No," she said. No other answer was forthcoming. Adelbert waited a second, then said,

"She doesn't do anything. She sits in her room and stares at the wall, except when I make her move."

Now I was alarmed. "What do you mean? She's only a young girl!" For her eyes were not those of a dullard, or even of a rebel. She was withdrawn, but she was not insane.

"Listen, you *Christian,* you!" Adelbert exclaimed, on his feet as he slammed an indignant fist onto the table. "Tam comes from a devout religious family. You know the works. So what happens when she gets into trouble? Do they stand by her? No! They make her sign away her baby, and then they kick her out!"

He quieted. "You think Christ is the answer to everything. Well, He's not! The biggest hypocrites in the world are Christians."

"You're mistaken!" I cried. "Everyone who calls himself a Christian isn't one. A Christian is a 'Christ-one' — a person who models himself after Christ. You can go through every kind of religious ritual and still not follow Christ. That's a matter of the heart. True Christianity involves a change of heart — that's why Jesus used the term 'born-again.' It is a literal re-birth with a new attitude and a new experience. Do you understand?"

"No. I don't believe it. You're a nice girl, Mrs. King, but totally unrealistic."

He picked up his precious papers and started for the door. "Come on, Tam. We'll see you later, Mrs. King. Be sure to tell your husband *she* was here with me. I'd hate to tangle with him."

Tam might as well have been watching a stage production, for she displayed no emotion at all — not embarrassment, or anger, or indignation. Surely she was aware of the conversation, but it might have concerned the extermination of Armadilloes, for all it involved her. In no mannerism did she remind me of Miriam, but still, a picture of that girl's desperate white face stabbed my memory.

CHAPTER SEVEN

Like coal miners emerging from their ebony pit at the end of a gruelling day, we anticipated our Sundays among God's people. It was our one day of quiet, when we could shut out the dissonant godlessness of those about us. Bruce never studied on Sunday afternoons. We either read or took long walks, for it was the only time in the week we had together when we were not rushed. We valued Sunday as a precious treasure.

Pat met us in the lobby of Trentwood Church that Sunday following her decision for Christ. With hands clasped loosely in her lap, her eyes never left the pulpit from start of sermon to finish. Outwardly serene, her inner agitation revealed itself only in the form of questions she asked while others milled about us, on their way home for Sunday dinner.

"What does Dr. McPherson mean by 'dedication of the home life'? I thought only ministers and missionaries were dedicated. With an unbelieving husband, how could I have a dedicated home?"

They were not easy questions to answer. "Pat, I have Mondays off from work. Come visit me in the morning, and we'll go over these things when we have more time," I urged.

After she had driven off in her new car, Bruce said, "The McPhersons have invited us to dinner today. Want to go?"

"Of course," I said. It was the only dinner invitation we had received since arriving in Sheldon.

It must have been a spur-of-the-moment invitation, for the McPherson home lay cluttered in all its Sunday morning haste. But it was a "people house"; not so neat as to be exacting, certainly well-kept in all necessities. Though considerably more expensively furnished than my parents' home, it had some of the same air of comfortable haphazardness.

Their youngest son, Norman, was nearly the age of my brother, Ronnie. A shy, slender lad, he was the complete bookworm. Should the boys have chanced to meet, they would have felt nothing but contempt for one another, for they shared no common interests. Norman appeared in the dining room only after being called three times, bolted his food, and excused himself before dessert was served. His parents dismissed him without comment. The boy seemed to be an afterthought in the busy household. I felt a little sorry for him, which sentiment, no doubt, would have amazed him. He had no inkling of pity for himself. He was one of those rare souls who genuinely preferred solitude.

I had helped make the salad and set the table before dinner. Now Bruce insisted it was his turn to assist in the kitchen. He donned an apron and proceeded to wash the dishes faster than Mrs. McPherson could wipe and put them away. It was rather novel, watching him, for he never did them at home. I wandered into the living room and sat fiddling at the old upright piano they had in the farthest corner.

"That's very nice," came Dr. McPherson's voice from behind my left shoulder. I hadn't heard him enter the room, and would never have ventured to touch the piano if I had thought anyone was listening. The venerable pastor was such a saint of God that I was never comfortable alone with him. His light blue eyes seemed able to read into a person's inmost thoughts, and my inmost thoughts were generally unworthy of note. I paused in the middle of a chord.

"I haven't played since last summer. I'm not very good."

"Sure you are. Did you know the junior department in Sunday school is looking for a pianist to play choruses for the opening exercises?"

"In a church this big? Surely you have lots of pianists!"

"Not willing pianists. People in Trentwood aren't much different from people in other churches — they're all willing to let George do it. Would you like to be our George?"

I thought a minute. "I never have a chance to practice. And choruses are harder to play than straight hymns, you know."

"You could come early to prayer meeting, or stay later, and practice on the church piano. We intend to tap Bruce for music, too – solos, male quartet, choir. It's time you two left your cocoon and joined the rest of the world."

"I — well, I didn't feel as if we were in a cocoon," I said, stammering a little in my haste to rearrange my thoughts. "We're busy all week. It's nice to take Sunday to relax."

"If we all relaxed on Sunday, when would the Lord's work ever be done?"

"Oh. Well, it's done by more experienced people than I."

He smiled. "Where do you suppose they got their experience? We also need a teacher for our fourth grade Sunday school girls. Think you could handle it?"

"I've never taught children that age."

"Fine. Then you'll enjoy the new experience."

I realized he was using high pressure methods to achieve what he was after. But he was so full of charm and love that I could not have formed the word "no" if I had wanted to. Actually, service was the one thing I missed in this large church. It had never occurred to me there was a lack of willing workers at Trentwood, where the teaching was so energetic, it seemed each member of the congregation should be inspired to go out and do something useful.

On the other hand, there was a problem with church work. Like the tentacles of an octopus, it gradually enmeshed one until there was not an evening in the week free of an activity. Pioneer Girls, Boys Brigade, Sunday school staff meetings, youth fellowship, choir practice, ladies' missionary groups — I had watched my parents in their involvement, and secretly vowed never to become thus occupied myself.

Bruce, of course, was more than willing to help with the music program of the church. He had probably only been waiting to be asked, for he grinned and remarked,

"Oh, now, Pastor McPherson, you didn't have to invite us home to dinner just to get us to say yes."

He *could* sing. His beautiful baritone voice would fill an auditorium till it reverberated from wall to wall, and the entire congregation was hushed to silent awe. He preferred music with quiet dignity, and he always put into it a quality of majesty which revealed his sincere appreciation of the meaning. No sloppy, offhand performance for him. Whether he sang for five or five hundred, he practiced, and memorized and polished.

His college professors promised he could have made a successful career in music. But he had chosen the more difficult one of medicine. And to it he applied the same devotion to perfection which would, in time, produce a first rate physician and surgeon.

The Sunday school of Trentwood Church was large enough for each department to have its own superintendent. Mrs. Stauffer was introduced to me as the superintendent of the junior department that evening. A short, dumpy woman given to wearing dresses of large floral print, she acknowledged her introduction to me with only the glimmer of a smile. Teaching was a very serious business with Mrs. Stauffer

"I have the material here, Mrs. King," she said in an uncommonly low voice, "but I would like to spend some time with you to be certain you understand the program of our Sunday school. When will you be free?"

"Oh, I'd love to have company." Even to my own ears, I sounded gushy. I finished more soberly, "I have Mondays off from work. Could you come in the afternoon?"

She nodded. "About two, then. Yes, I know where Prospect Street is."

She turned to more important matters, keeping the precious Sunday school material safe in her own hands.

I anticipated a busy day, but Pat did not come in the morning as she had tentatively agreed to do. Perhaps some appointment she had forgotten — we had no phone for her to call.

Exactly at two (I wondered if she had driven around the block in order to hit the minute absolutely right), Mrs. Stauffer knocked at my door. With her she had her youngest child, a boy of five.

"My name is Mark," he announced, with none of his mother's gravity. "Where's your toy box?"

"Oh, Mark, I'm sorry," I said. "We don't have a toy box. Would you like a cookie?"

He shrugged indifferently. "Okay. Can I watch TV?"

He helped himself to a cookie and looked about the room, his lively tongue never quiet for an instant.

"We don't have TV, either, Mark. You could listen to the radio in my bedroom if you keep it down low."

"Nothing good on the radio," remarked this sophisticated child of the world. "Do you have any records? I like Pinocchio."

"I'm sorry, Mark." (Apparently, I was going to spend my afternoon telling Mark I was sorry.) "We don't even have a record player."

He wrinkled his little turned-up nose. "You don't have nothin'. Are you poor?"

"Not really. I have some magazines. Would you like to look at them?"

He agreed, though his heart wasn't in it. During the exchange, his mother wisely kept silent. When Mark finally settled down to a listless perusal of adult literature, Mrs. Stauffer opened our talk with prayer.

She seemed a very spiritual woman, intensely desirous of seeing her young charges come into a knowledge of Jesus as Saviour. Point by point, she explained the lesson to me — far more thoroughly than Mrs. Stibbe had done when I taught in Harbrook Academy. Her voice was monotonous, and I found myself lulled into a drowsiness I could hardly fight. Mark wandered about the room, opening drawers to inspect their contents. His mother did not reprove him. Since he was doing no real harm, I said nothing, either. He must have been dreadfully bored. I wondered how many times a week he was subjected to this type of recreation.

When each detail of the quarter's lesson plans had been discussed to Mrs. Stauffer's satisfaction, I served tea and cookies. Mark bustled eagerly to the table, not because he was hungry, but because any change was welcome.

"Quiet, Mark, and we'll thank Jesus for the food," said Mrs. Stauffer. I was somewhat taken aback. I had always thought the hostess made the move to say grace.

Mark was more interested in telling me about the warts on his fingers.

"Be quiet, Mark," said his mother sternly. "We want to tell Jesus that we love Him."

"I don't," returned Mark in a jaunty manner.

"Of course you do. We all love Jesus."

"No. I don't," said Mark. "Daddy doesn't. The bread man doesn't. The milkman doesn't. The policeman doesn't."

The list of people who didn't love Jesus threatened to be endless. Fearing I would titter and ruin my reputation forever, I bowed my head and said a hasty grace.

Mrs. Stauffer saw nothing humorous in the little boy's rebellion. She had seemed on the point of treating his childish statement as open heresy. If she conducted all her household incidents with such seriousness, what kind of tension existed there?

In any church, some few always catch the visitor's eye as leaders. Mrs. Stauffer was such a one. Even before she became my superintendent, I had noticed her. Her husband, vice-president in charge of something-or-other at the mill, was never in church. Her two teen-age daughters were outrageously flirtatious, even to my half-tolerant eye. There were also two boys older than Mark, but I had not yet focused on them.

After she had gone, I lay down on the couch, completely exhausted. I couldn't understand my fatigue. Something about straining to hear her low, monotonous voice, or struggling to keep awake. Then it struck me! Mrs. Stauffer didn't know the major from the minor. Each circumstance was treated with equally painstaking care. If she cleaned drawers and closets with such thoroughness, how did she ever get to the rest of the house?

Once I had agreed to teach the fourth grade girls, I looked forward eagerly to the experience. The material was excellent, well-laid out, and each minute accounted for. With adequate preparation, a novice could teach these lessons with no difficulty.

I needn't have worried about my piano-playing. The opening exercises included only enough time for two simple choruses. Then Mrs. Stauffer launched into a fifteen-minute discourse entitled, "Bible Lands in Bible Times." Thoroughly prepared, the geography lesson was informative, but completely unsuitable to this age group. Like the lecturer, it was very good, but very dull. The restless children shot spitballs at one another, while a dozen teachers tried to keep unobtrusive order.

My class of eleven girls proved, not so much challenging, as appealing. They were typical youngsters from middle-class homes, well-dressed, half-way mannerly, not yet interested in boys. In spiritual knowledge, they ranged from totally ignorant to very well-indoctrinated. Inasmuch as I was a new teacher, they gave me their undivided attention. This would not last, I knew.

Betty Thurston met me in the hall after the dismissal bell had rung. She taught the fifth grade girls.

"How did you like the lecture at the beginning?" she inquired with a mischievously innocent grin. Betty was so plain, she was cute. Not more than five feet tall, with wrists and ankles small as a child's, a pug nose over slightly protruding teeth which wrinkled in nervous expressiveness, to give her the look of a female Bugs Bunny, she had the gift of laughter — and it was never cruel.

"Does she do this every week?" I inquired, quite concerned.

"No. She tries to vary the opening exercises. She's only been superintendent a month. Before that, she taught for years and years, until her classes dwindled down to just the kids who were forced to attend. She's a good woman, Sandy, and a hard worker. We didn't want to hurt her by taking her class away from her, so we department teachers voted to kick her upstairs."

"I hope you don't lose any more kids. That was ghastly!"

"Well, it only lasts fifteen minutes. Then we teachers have to make up for it by being doubly interesting in class."

It was, of course, the expedient solution. How many institutions outside the church would promote a person for exceptionally poor performance?

Even in church, Pat's beauty caused mild sensation. She sat beside us every morning, impeccably robed in the latest fashion. Still, she managed to forget her appearance as easily as we plainer women did, and concentrated fiercely on every word Dr. Mc-Pherson uttered.

In the church bulletin one Sunday was printed an appeal for help in the nursery department during the Sunday school hour. I merely glanced at it, not even taking in the words, but as soon as the benediction had been spoken, Pat poked me with her elbow.

"Sandy, do you think they'd let me help in the nursery?" Like almost everything she said, there was an undertone of earnestness to Pat's question. I often felt she weighed each statement carefully before uttering it. She had been tremendously impressed when I told her I was going to teach Sunday school — almost as if I had attained unbelievable heights of spiritual enlightenment. Pat was not a girl to try to outdo another — she only wanted to find a place of service in this lively, bustling fellowship of believers.

"I think they'd be delighted with a volunteer. I'll suggest it tomorrow night at the Sunday school teacher's meeting," I promised.

Outside, she squinted in the sun. "Where's your car parked?" she asked. "I don't see it."

Bruce hesitated briefly. "We sold it, Pat. We don't need it in the city."

She appeared stunned, as if we had announced we were down to eating dog food. "How are you going to get home?" she asked.

"Bus. They run every half hour."

"Oh, let me take you home. Don's playing golf this morning."

She accepted our invitation to dinner with no hesitation. Her marriage, perhaps, was no odder than many, but it struck us as a strange husband-and-wife relationship. They seemed hardly to let the right hand know what the left was doing. Pat had not yet summoned up courage to tell Don she had accepted the Lord as Saviour, or that she was going to church with us.

They spent one evening a week regularly with each other, at the Club on Friday night. Saturday Don recuperated from his hangover, and lounged around the house. Sunday they went their separate ways — Don "out with the boys," usually playing golf. Pat was left to her own devices, and not expected to complain. She had her own car and her own friends. The emptiness of their marriage caused me literal pain.

There was little for Pat to do in her own home, for she employed a full time maid. She was free to roam as she pleased.

Women's clubs and charity organizations interested her less and less as time went on. And yet she was careful not to impose on our time together. Instead of spending Sunday afternoons with us, she returned on Monday mornings to talk to me while I worked around the house.

Always the conversation turned to spiritual topics. Pat's ignorance of the most basic Christian tenets was heart-tearing. Her hunger for knowledge far outdistanced mine. She was dangerously open to any and all ideas parading under the term of "religion."

She asked about reincarnation, Joseph Smith, the earthly kingdom, and mind control. I had to borrow books from the McPhersons to answer questions I had never thought to ask myself. If Pat received nothing from these studies, I learned a great deal. As much as possible, I directed her queries to the Word of God. Starting with Matthew, we read together of the life of Jesus. And for the first time, I began to perceive the complexity of His sermon on the mount. The beautifully balanced cadences had always struck my ear as lovely poetry; now, with Pat, I began to wonder at the meaning. Who are the meek? The pure in heart? How could they inherit the earth? Would they want to?

The more I tried to answer Pat's queries, the more I questioned on my own. "Feasting on the Word of God" had always struck me as a terribly old-fashioned phrase. Now I knew what it meant. Like a sumptuous banquet, the more we "ate," the more there was to eat.

I have never liked staff meetings. If it had not been for Pat's wish to help in the Sunday school nursery, I would have skipped this one. Perhaps it would have been better if I had. For, from past experience, I knew that Christian brethren did not always dwell together peaceably. And in staff meetings, their disagreements were most likely to surface.

I found a seat at the long table beside Betty Thurston. Her sly asides brightened the dreariest sessions. Across from us, and a little down, Mrs. Stauffer smiled in benevolence. Nothing at this meeting was of special interest — curtains for the new addition, special music for Mother's day from the junior choir, plans for summer Vacation Bible School. It was an efficient church, run along the lines of a well-planned business. Each worker knew where his duties lay. If he was incapacitated, there would always be another to step in.

When the meeting opened for miscellaneous business, I thought it the proper opportunity to offer Pat's services to the nursery supervisor. Some day, perhaps, I'll learn to feel my way carefully before blundering. I could have asked Betty Thurston the proper procedure, for this was not a topic for general discussion. I know it now, but I didn't know it then.

A little frown crossed Mrs. Stauffer's face when my suggestion dropped itself in the room. "Who is this young lady?" she asked. "Is she the worldly-looking girl who sat beside you yesterday morning?"

"Worldly looking?" I repeated, as I frantically tried to think what Pat had worn to fit the description of "worldly-looking." A loose-fitting lavender suit, certainly less garish than the blue and green flowered jersey acetate Mrs. Stauffer had on at the moment. What were these standards of worldliness, anyway? Mrs. Stauffer's daughters sported a different shade of blonde every month!

"Perhaps that wasn't a good choice of words," Mrs. Stauffer admitted in her gravelly voice. "I'm very anxious to see that all our workers are born-again Christians. Are you certain your sister-in-law is saved?"

I kept my voice calm, explaining, "She's made a start. Her husband isn't interested in the Lord, and Pat doesn't feel she can make a public confession of faith without angering him. She needs to grow, and I know it would help her if she felt a part of the church."

"We're sympathetic with your feelings, Mrs. King," she said, as if she had conferred with all the Sunday school teachers and was now their appointed spokesman. "But we cannot endanger our children's spiritual welfare by placing them under the tutelage of an uncertain teacher."

By this time, I was thoroughly confused. "I didn't understand you wanted a *teacher!* I thought you needed someone to help with the *babies!*"

"Yes," spoke up a younger woman from farther down the table. I gathered she was the nursery supervisor. "She wouldn't be teaching, Mrs. Stauffer. And she wouldn't be in *charge* of the nursery. We need steady, reliable help every Sunday. We'd like to have the same assistants as much as possible so the children become accustomed to them. Then they don't cry when their mothers leave them."

Mrs. Stauffer's lips drew together in disapproval. "It isn't this specific person, so much as the principle," she stated with ponderous emphasis. "If we allow an unsaved woman to help here, what would prevent her from teaching older children at some later date? If we break down our standards, we will lose our reason for existence. We'll become like all the other churches in town — liberal and unsanctified."

If poor Pat had any idea of the threat she posed to these innocent babies, she would have gone out and drowned herself. Then and there, I determined to keep her from any staff meetings for years to come.

"I'm sorry," I said, "for having stirred up such a bee's nest. But as long as we're on the subject, I think you shouldn't print requests for volunteers in the church bulletin, if you're going to be so rigid about your workers. It's going to be embarrassing for me to tell Pat you don't want her help after she offered it."

Betty bumped her knee against mine. Apparently this particular matter was a very sore bone of contention.

"I agree," said Mrs. Stauffer. "It should not have gone in the bulletin. Since your sister-in-law is such a young Christian, she ought to be attending Adult Class in Sunday school, rather than helping with babies, where she doesn't learn anything. I feel very strongly that we should have only sanctified workers in our church."

There was that word again — "sanctified." Each little group seemed to have its own connotation for it. Webster defines it as "the state of holiness." Some of my friends at Harbrook thought it meant abstinence from wearing jewelry and makeup. Others considered it a state of sinless perfection. Some preferred the terms "dedication" or "consecration." And a few older people in my home church thought it meant the privilege of sitting in judgment on other, struggling Christians. I remembered back, not so long ago, to my teen years. An old deacon in the church, short of stature and long on words, spent all his spare breath chiding us on our lack of "sanctification." He perhaps could not distinguish it from sanctimony.

He could pray for twenty minutes at a stretch, all around the world and back to the "worldly young people in our own church." My parents considered him a "real prayer warrior." What we young people considered him was better not expressed.

When, after a semester at college, I accepted the Lord, this old deacon shook my hand warmly. "I prayed you into the kingdom of God," he intoned piously.

My whole backbone stiffened. If credit were given in Heaven, I hoped he would not share in it. It had been *in spite* of him, certainly not *because* of him, that any of us had been saved. These older people, so delighted with a new-born infant, could allow him to grow physically at his own pace. But when it came to a new-born Christian, they expected Instant Maturity, with none of the stumblings they had experienced themselves.

The general superintendent had cleared his throat for attention, and I made a hasty transition from Bartlett to Trentwood.

"Perhaps we could table this for another time," he suggested diplomatically. I wished I had kept quiet. Of one thing I was resolved — no more Sunday school teachers' meetings for me!

Betty walked down the corridor with me. She was delightful company, and if she hadn't lived across town from us, would have been close friends. She steered carefully away from the subject she knew was boiling within me.

"Mrs. King," a voice called, just as we reached the doorway. It was the nursery supervisor. Betty walked on outside, for her husband was waiting for her.

"Could you give me your sister-in-law's phone number?"

"Are you going to ask her, after all this?" I asked in amazement.

"Oh, certainly," the supervisor smiled sweetly. "If we tried to keep everyone happy all of the time, we never would get the Lord's work done."

"I'm sorry I blundered into this. It was very foolish of me. Will Mrs. Stauffer . . . ?"

"It really isn't up to Mrs. Stauffer to worry about the nursery," replied the supervisor. I liked her better with every minute. "I'm the one who needs the help."

For every Christian who balks at each suggestion as if it were a bone to be worried to death, there are always ten others to move along in perfect smoothness, paying attention to the essentials in life.

CHAPTER EIGHT

It had been one of those made-in-March days, when the weather could not make up its mind to be kind or cruel. Farther north, snow still blanketed the ground. Farther south, buds had already formed on the trees. But here, in Sheldon, depressing skies and muddy terrain were the best the month had produced. So when the knock sounded on the apartment door, my heart surged with hope for diversion of any kind.

I opened the door, then stepped back with a startled gasp. The figure in the hallway looked like nothing less than an abandoned field mouse. It was short — not even up to my shoulders — and female. In her tiny, claw-like hand she carried a bag made up of faded strips of carpeting sewn together in a valiant attempt to simulate a cross between a purse and a brief case. Her clothes, though not ragged, had been scavenged from some forgotten attic trunk. Her silk dress, originally black, had turned to rust with age. From under the heavily fringed olive shawl draped across her shoulders extended long black sleeves with useless silk-covered buttons marching in single file to the elbows. Her bonnet, indescribably horrid, was tied beneath her chin in an enormous purple bow. For some reason, the ribbon had retained its color, while all the other clothing had faded into varied shades of anemic drabness. Under the floor-length skirt peeped two tiny doll's feet in scuffed black shoes. The hall was permeated with a peculiar odor of must, moth balls, and lavender sachet.

The skin on her hands and face sagged as if the little lady had recently lost a great deal of weight. Her peaked nose quivered every time her lips moved, which was constantly. She was peering shortsightedly at the name card tacked outside our door. When she looked up, her dark eyes gleamed innocently. There was not a question but what she would be welcome.

"King — yes, that's the name, Bruce King — my, aren't you a nice young thing — so fresh and pretty — may I come in?"

She had already crossed the threshold, and I found myself backing in reluctant amazement as the tiny figure entered our living room, not waiting for an invitation.

"My, haven't you a pretty little place here — you'd never know it from the outside — isn't it a shame the way this neighborhood has run down — I do think the mayor should do something, don't you — but what can you expect of a Democrat — my husband always said they were full of hot air — do you mind if I sit down — these old feet get tired and . . . ."

Already dropped on the couch, she paused long enough to take in the surroundings. Her entire monologue had been delivered without pause or punctuation. Now she rummaged in her carpet bag and from its muddled depths produced a pamphlet.

My stomach tightened in mild tension as I took it from the spidery hand, for religious cultists were creatures I could not fathom. I always suspected they secretly hoped I would be condemned, if for nothing better than to prove themselves right.

The paper turned out to be, instead, a badly-blurred advertisement for some magic vitamin known as Nutri-Life. A quick perusal told me that if one took three tablets daily for three months, he would find himself so healthy, he could practically go without eating. There was no mention of price.

The little saleslady had continued to talk, but I deduced it was only to fill a vacuum of silence. Her discourse seemed to have no bearing on the product. Though I realized I could not afford the vitamins if they had been given away free, I felt obliged for the sake of courtesy to give the matter some consideration.

"How much does it cost?"

The beady eyes stared blankly. "Cost?" Her pointed tongue darted in and out, moistening her lips. "Oh, the Nutri-Life!"

She acted as if she had been dragged from the abstract to the mundane against her will. "You don't have to take three daily if you don't want to. You could take two or even one, and it wouldn't cost you so much."

I couldn't resist a grin. "Or none at all, and it wouldn't cost me anything."

The saleslady missed the barb. She launched into a recital of her own medical history, doubtless meaning to lead up to the marvelous healing powers of Nutri-Life, but she never quite arrived. It was a rambling portrayal, not without its own element of drama, in which all her internal organs were described as vividly as characters in a soap opera.

"Doctor Levi — you know, the father, not the son, these young men never know what they're doing and they haven't time for a cup of tea — he said he'd never *seen* such a gall bladder as mine. And when he got to the spleen — it was that big and puffy — when I came out from the ether he said, 'Celia Rosequist, I'm surprised you're still alive.' "

Here she paused to await my comment, breathing in delighted pleasure at our shared adventure. I smiled and thought how lucky I was not to be squeamish.

"Would you like a cup of tea?" I asked, for want of a better remark.

The little lady's eyelids dropped to cover her eagerness, while her chin quivered suddenly. "Now, don't put yourself to any trouble," she replied, in a tone which implied, "Please hurry. I'm famished."

Smitten with pity, I wondered how long it had been since

she'd eaten a decent meal. There were no baked goods in the cupboard. I placed some graham crackers on a small plate on the table while the tea water was heating. Mrs. Rosequist eased herself over to the table and ate four, non-stop, before I could pour the tea. I was aghast. What was the welfare department in Sheldon doing? Why did an ancient little lady have to peddle vitamins for a living? I wracked my brain to think of some excuse to keep her in the apartment while I slipped out to a pay phone to ask for help. But then, Bruce would be home in a half-hour. He could find a better solution.

Over the tea, Mrs. Rosequist's memory was revived, along with her spirits. She apparently had lived in the neighborhood all her life, for, when she had completed the minute details of her physical condition, she proceeded into the lengthy history of each of the town's leading families. I had no way of knowing what was sheer fantasy or what was based on truth. The visitor never disclosed the sources of her information; it was more like an eyewitness account. Greed, murder, scandal all rolled off her tongue as merrily as Tales from Chaucer.

As if my landlady were lurking within earshot, she confessed to a long-standing feud with Mrs. Ajarian, in a sharp whisper.

"Mary Ajarian is filthy rich, you know," she said with a grin devoid of malice.

"Really?" I asked skeptically. I had seen the interior of Mrs. Ajarian's tiny apartment behind her store. Nothing indicating luxury dwelt within.

"She keeps her money in the hollow of her wooden leg. You did know she had a wooden leg? It happened in an accident with a horse. She doesn't like me because I stole her best beau when we were young. Oh, but I was a beauty! Coal black hair, snow white skin, and the prettiest eyes you ever did see. None of the young men could resist me — I was that pretty. But then, neither of us married him, and he became a minister."

Mrs. Rosequist clasped her hands before her in an attitude of reverence and sighed deeply. I had a mental picture of the young man, stricken with grief, retiring into the ministry as his only solace.

"Two things I love," she continued. "I love to go to church, and I love to go to the doctor."

My stomach ached from suppressed laughter. Darling Mrs. Rosequist! She would never know how she had brightened a dismal day!

Outside, it was growing dark. The door opened, and Bruce

stepped into the room, blinking in the lamp's glow. He frowned as if he could not quite believe his eyes. I stepped to his side and gently squeezed his elbow to warn him to be careful with his ejaculations.

The faded rose on top of her ghastly hat bobbing in rhythm with her tongue, Mrs. Rosequist rose to her feet and advanced to meet him, as if she were the hostess and he the guest.

"So happy to meet you, Mr. Bruce. I am Celia Rosequist. Would you have a cup of tea with us?"

"Thank you," he replied, still somewhat befuddled. "I think I'll get washed up for dinner."

I excused myself briefly to follow Bruce into the cubbyhole of a bedroom.

"Bruce, I think she's hungry. Shall I invite her to dinner?"

"Who is she? One of your relatives?"

I nodded. "I didn't dare invite her to the wedding, for fear you'd back out." I spoiled my joke by giggling. "No, she's selling Nutri-Life."

"What's Nutri-Life?"

I whispered rapidly, "She's terribly poor. See if you can get her address so we can get some help from the welfare department. You'll have to give up one of your potatoes. I only baked three."

"I can fill up on bread. What's Nutri-Life?"

"I'd better get back out there, or she'll think we're talking about her."

"Aren't we? What's Nutri-Life?"

I blew him a kiss from the doorway and returned to our visitor. She had retired to the questionable comfort of the couch to observe my preparations without once expressing doubt as to her own invitation to share the meal. I began to wonder if the little soul planned to stay overnight with us.

Bruce came out of the bathroom, his shirt open at the neck, and the stiffness gone from his bearing. He often found odd people difficult, but as time went on, he improved. He set the table for three while I pulled the meatloaf and potatoes from the oven, opened a can of peas and cut carrot and celery sticks.

Mrs. Rosequist resumed her role of hostess, indicating where Bruce and I were to sit, then taking the head of the table for herself. In her cloudy mind, she had become once more the charming mistress of a well-run home. I seemed to have been relegated to the role of poor relation, allowed to eat with the family, but expected to do the fetching and clearing. Bruce, Mrs.

Rosequist set about to entertain. As if they were still alive, she told him tales of her contemporaries (leaving out all the scandalous details which I had heard earlier), she asked his advice on stock investment and insurance policies. Unaccustomed to this flattering reliance on his financial sagacity, Bruce grinned with the fixed smile of an overgrown kewpie doll, answering only in monosyllables.

The meal over, Mrs. Rosequist excused herself to go into the bathroom. Even then we could hear her muttering through the thin door. Bruce put his arms around me from behind, to kiss the back of my neck.

"I love to come home to you. I never know what I'm going to find," he chuckled.

Rocked by silent laughter, we swayed in each other's arms.

"We'll have to find where she lives," he whispered a moment later. "Whoever she lives with is going to be worried."

"Oh, do you think she lives with someone? I thought she had a grubby little attic room with no one to talk to but a moulting parrot."

"Is that what she told you?"

"No. It's what I pictured."

"Oh. I think the two of you would make a pretty good pair."

More than ever resembling a tiny field mouse, Mrs. Rosequist came out of the bathroom, still talking. Bruce took a step forward, interrupting her ceaseless chit-chat for the first time.

"Mrs. Rosequist, I'll be glad to walk you home, or call a cab for you. Could you tell me where you live?"

She looked about to cry. Her wrinkled chin quivered, and her beady eyes squinted like a child's. "Oh, is it time to go so soon?"

Then, suddenly, another mood was upon her. She smiled and held out her hand in a gracious gesture. "I've *so* enjoyed your visit. Do come again."

Bruce was very patient. "Yes, you can come again. But we must get you home. Did you wear a coat?"

I picked up the shawl from the couch, where our visitor had discarded it, and laid it gently across the old lady's shoulders. Without argument, Mrs. Rosequist stuffed her Nutri-Life pamphlet into the odoriferous carpet bag and started for the door on such quick little feet that Bruce and I had to run to catch up with her.

The weather was giving its typical early March performance. Not as bitter cold as it had been a month ago, still it was raw and very windy. There was no moon, and the streets were dark, for neighborhood gangs had been on the loose and broken half the street lights.

"Which way, Mrs. Rosequist?" Bruce asked, as he took her arm.

"Oh, I can find my own way," she replied vaguely.

"No. We'll take you. What's your address?"

She became deliberately evasive. "It's just a couple of blocks away. I prefer to go by myself."

Bruce's voice took on that little-used note of authority. "We'll go with you. Which way?"

We started off to the right for two blocks. Then Mrs. Rosequist directed us across the street and to the left for three blocks. Then it was left again, with the little lady rambling in fragmentary chatter. I was cold, and wondered if Mrs. Rosequist's constant exercise of her tongue provided enough stimulation to keep her entire body warm. We weren't really back-tracking, for the roads were not laid out perfectly straight, but we were not heading for any exact destination by the most direct route. We were more than a mile from our own tenement, and seemingly no closer to Mrs. Rosequist's.

"Are you sure you know the way, Mrs. Rosequist?" Bruce asked.

"Of course I know the way. Are you getting tired, young man? I can go on by myself. It isn't far."

"What's the address? It seems we've been wandering without getting anywhere."

"This is the way I always go. I like to look in the shop windows. My, don't they have pretty dresses now. But too short. My mother always used to say, 'Celia, keep your ankles covered. Save them for your husband's eyes.' I always did have pretty ankles, slender and nice. But when I got married, do you know, my husband never noticed. I thought how foolish I had been to . . . ."

A car pulled to the curb beside us and a bright light shone directly on us. A policeman stepped from the car and inspected our startled faces.

"Yep, it's her," he called to his companion. "You can turn off the light."

He addressed Bruce in an overbearing tone. "Where ya headin', mister?"

Bruce, whose tolerance for authority in uniform was extremely low, replied testily, "We're trying to escort this lady to her home."

"Well, you're goin' the wrong way. D'ya know who she is?"

"She says she's Celia Rosequist."

"That's right. She's been missin' since early morning. Why didn't ya report her? The notice has been on all the radio stations."

"I've been in class all day. I didn't listen to the news." Bruce's exasperation was beginning to show. I began to wonder if policemen were trained to treat civilians as guilty until proven innocent. But guilty of what? What possible wrong could there be in walking along the street with a poverty-stricken old lady, even if it was dark?

"Yeah?" The policeman showed his disbelief. "How much money did she give you?"

Mrs. Rosequist broke in with her little field mouse squeal. "Oh, my, how could I forget? I did want to give you some money, and this nice gentleman just reminded me."

She opened her carpet bag and from its depths pulled a wad of rumpled green bills. "I don't know how much this is. Will it be enough?"

Bruce pushed her hand back into the carpet bag. "Thank you, Mrs. Rosequist. It was a pleasure to meet you. But we don't need your money."

"I know you don't need it. You have so much already. But, please, it's all I can do for people I like." She dropped her voice and whispered conspiratorially, "I have lots more at home."

The policeman's voice took on the respect one accords to another of superior funds. "Mrs. Rosequist, let me drive you home. Your daughter is worried."

"Oh, I'd love to ride in the police car. And would you turn on the siren? Do you remember when I went to the hospital? A hundred miles an hour we went. It's a pity I wasn't feeling well enough to enjoy it."

Still talking, Mrs. Rosequist settled herself in the back seat of the police car and was driven off. The siren remained silent.

Bruce and I watched as the tail light became a red dot in the distance. We were stupefied into a temporary dumbness. Then I exploded in a shriek. "Oh, Bruce! I suppose she'll turn out to be the richest woman in the city! And I was all set to go home and call the welfare department! Do you think she really sells Nutri-Life?"

He grunted. "How much did she sell you? I think she was

just using it as an excuse to get into your apartment. She probably smelled you a mile away."

"But those people she was talking about! Are they real?"

"Maybe. I've heard some of their names."

"Could they really have been as bad as she said?"

"I don't know what she said before I got there. But you know what I think? I think most of this is an act. She may be a little daft, but — oh, come on. I've got to study."

CHAPTER NINE

Glowering March gave way to affable April. Tiny patches of earth offered yellow and purple crocuses for color, the sun ventured forth in timid glory, and the residents of dingy Prospect Street pulled out of their shells long enough to smile in relief from the long winter's loneliness. Life was a round of narrow activity — work, church, home and Pat. We never went anywhere and rarely saw anyone different.

Several times, I tried attending the Young Married Women's Missionary Circle. But conversation centered mainly on baby food and diaper rash, two subjects in which I had no interest. One thing I learned from these young mothers, however — no one was really interested in anyone else's baby. They simply waited politely for the chance to tell about theirs. I loved Betty Thurston, and could have been close friends with her — until she, too, began describing the symptoms of morning sickness and strange eating desires. I pretended interest, but secretly, I felt she had betrayed me in joining the ranks of expectant motherhood. It was a state which would be denied me for many years yet.

At work, the tips were good, and Mr. Mylan favored me as the best waitress he had had in years. It did not set too well with my co-workers, any more than a teacher showing favoritism in class sets well with other children. As "teacher's pet" I was excluded from the kitchen jokes. Actually, I was innocent enough not to understand some of them, and to be shocked at others. The maître d' was a poisonous little man, with a grudge against all cheerful people. He snapped at me on every flimsy excuse. Gradually, through the months of waitressing, I learned to detach myself, to observe these little frictions as if I were not involved. It was good training experience, I realized, though certainly there should have been more pleasant occupations.

Then, one day in mid-April, Don King came into the restaurant. My stomach churned in a lump of anxiety, for with him was, not his wife, but a black-haired girl in a skirt so tight she could barely hobble. They were seated at a table near the entrance, with Don's back toward me, leaving me ample opportunity to verify his identity. I hated myself for spying, but it seemed unavoidable. Apparently Pat had not told him I worked there. Surely he would not be brazen enough to bring another woman to lunch under a relative's nose. For whatever else could be said about Mr. King's ideas, he was a rigidly moral man. He would not countenance "affairs" or divorce. If word ever reached his ears that his nephew was stepping out of line, Don would be cut off from the family fortune as surely as Bruce had been.

I tried to convince myself that this was only a business luncheon. But instinct said it was not so. Don's hand covered the girl's on the linen tablecloth, she stared into his eyes with the rapt expression of a thirteen-year-old watching a long-haired quartet. It was no innocent chance meeting, and I wanted to bash the man's head against the wall.

Sweet, beautiful Pat, with the lustrous eyes and inquiring soul. How could Don *do* such a thing to her? What terrible breakdown in communications could have caused so great a catastrophe? They had been married less than two years — he couldn't be bored with his wife so soon!

I thought back, looking for clues. Pat spoke of Don seldom, and it had struck me that they spent little time together. But this was the way of sophisticates.

There were customers to satisfy. By the time I had filled their orders and returned to the dining room, Don and his friend were gone. My mind in a daze, I performed my duties mechanically, with no remembrance of them later.

I longed to talk to Bruce. But he was in the midst of mid-term exams, and studying like a madman. A shock like this could only disturb, and not help. He dearly loved Pat, and his anger against his brother would be fierce. No human help was available, and I could only pray that Don would come to his senses before Pat wakened to the situation. Urbane and blasé as some pretend to be, infidelity cuts a wound almost too deep to heal. Pat was neither urbane nor blasé.

The problem worried me, late into the night. If I went to Don's office and confronted him with my knowledge, would it churn trouble, or dissolve it?

Somehow, I managed to put the distress aside when Bruce came home. If I smiled only wanly at his conversation, he appeared not to notice. His studies absorbed his total interest. And though I failed to find anything interesting in the structure of the muscular system, I was glad he was distracted from his former keen powers of observation.

Don and his friend appeared no more in Alphand's. I convinced myself it was only a temporary fling, for Pat evidenced no signs of unaccustomed strain when she visited. Still, I wondered. Why had she never invited us to her ultra-modern home? We had seen it in the process of construction, but never completed. Did she reason the contrast between her dwelling and ours was too sharp? It hardly seemed explanation enough. More likely, she feared Don's wrath, if he discovered she were going to church with us.

I caught myself trying to read subtle meaning into each of the girl's statements. If there was a link, I could not find it. No, Pat did not know of Don's philandering, and possibly I suffered from an over-active imagination myself!

Alphand's was only five or six blocks from King's Department Store. It was a restaurant which catered to well-lined pocket books, and it was inevitable that some day Mr. King would walk through that door. Still, the surprise hit me like a glass of cold water.

He was with a group of businessmen — prosperous gentlemen who accepted their financial success as their just due. Our dining room was large, and there were any number of tables closer to the door for them to sit. Mr. Mylan, wanting to give me the best tips, led them straight to my set. I held my breath, but none of the men even glanced at my face.

Hoping not to attract Mr. King's attention in any way, I even omitted the customary "Good morning, gentlemen." I poured their water and handed them each a menu. Perhaps, if I had had the forethought to turn my engagement ring inward, I would have escaped notice. But I never thought of it.

The ring was a family heirloom, handed down from eldest

son to eldest son. It was valuable, though no one had ventured a monetary estimation. Just a year ago, Mr. King had had the diamond reset in a more modern ring to suit my simpler tastes. He recognized it instantly.

His eye struck my left hand, then traveled rapidly upward to my face. He flashed a warning glance at me, then, with a reddened face, he turned silently back to his companions, putting me definitely in my place. It hurt more than a slap in the face.

Their meal served, the men sat and talked and smoked while potential customers stood behind the ropes waiting for a table. No one ordered dessert. I poured second cups of coffee around, and I wished they would leave. Still, they lingered.

I returned from the kitchen, carrying a heavy tray. When I set it down on the big waitress' table, and turned, Mr. King stood at my elbow.

"What time will you be finished here today?" he asked.

"About three."

"Very well. Come out through the lobby. Tom will meet you and bring you to my office. I'd like to talk with you."

He turned on his well-polished heel and left. The summons, without so much as a by-your-leave, annoyed me to the point that I considered ignoring it. Still, for a week last year, we had been good friends. For no other reason, I decided to go see the old man.

At three, I put on my coat, passed through the dining room and into the lobby. Tom stood against a wall, in his chauffeur's uniform. A smile creased his brown friendly face as he met me halfway.

"Hello, Miss Sandra. How are you?"

He shook my hand cordially, and I relaxed in the warmth of his greeting. I was more at home with the servant than the employer.

"We're both fine, Tom. How's Ellen?"

He grinned even wider. Ellen was his wife. "Ellen hasn't changed in the last fifteen years. Still as cantankerous as ever."

Tom guided me outside to the waiting limousine. But instead of holding the back door for me, as he had done a year ago, he opened the front door. Becoming a waitress had won me this concession.

In the five minutes it took Tom to drive me to King's, I squeezed in what news of Bruce I could manage, for Tom and Ellen had maintained a closer relationship with Bruce and Don than their uncle had. The old are always more interested in the young than the young are in the old. It had been thoughtless of

Bruce not to give Tom and Ellen a call in their own home when he first arrived in Sheldon. They deserved at least that courtesy!

Tom parked the black Lincoln in Mr. King's reserved parking space and conducted me through the employee's entrance, into self-service elevator, and up to the fifth floor. From a brief glimpse into the main areas, I could see the various departments were preparing to greet spring in a galaxy of artificial apple blossoms and yellow forsythia. It was a lovely store. I wished I could afford to shop there.

In the corridor, we walked behind a young woman in a tight checked skirt. The swing of the hips and the careless toss of her head stirred a submerged memory. When she opened a door on which gilt letters spelled, "Mr. Donald King," I started and glanced back. It was, of course, the same girl he had wined and dined a few weeks before at Alphand's.

Tom noted my backward glance and asked, "Want to look in on Don? He'll be glad to see you."

I shook my head. "I'm not so sure."

Tom was at my elbow every second until we stood at Mr. King's inner door, almost as if he had been ordered not to let me out of his sight. The battery of girls typing in the outer office paid us no attention, but the steely-eyed receptionist nodded at Tom and said, "Go right in."

I turned the knob, and a cold chill of apprehension shivered through me. With a silent prayer, I entered.

Mr. King was at his shiny mahogany desk, staring out the window. A sheaf of papers lay before him, but they were far from his thoughts. And in that brief second, before he rose to greet me, I realized he had aged ten years. The strain of separation had been harder on him than on Bruce.

"Well, Sandra," Mr. King said with a pleasant smile, "and how are you?"

He held out his hand, and I took it, suddenly overwhelmed.

"Fine, Uncle Larry. And you?"

"Getting back on my feet gradually. I was ill this winter, and it takes an old man time to recuperate, you know."

"Uncle Larry!" I cried. "Why didn't someone tell us? We've been in Sheldon since February. Pat never breathed a word!"

His eyebrows rose. "Pat? Are you seeing her?"

Pat's reasons for secrecy escaped me. I decided to be honest. "Why, yes. She found our address in February, and comes almost every week for a visit. Didn't you know?"

"I had no idea." He dropped the subject abruptly. "Tell

me, why are you working in a restaurant? I thought you were planning to teach school."

"I was, but the school board had other ideas. Apparently they haven't heard of the teacher shortage. Anyway, I make more money as a waitress and I never have to correct papers at night."

"Do you like it?"

I smiled. "I prefer it to starvation."

He shook his head in resigned disgust. "I never thought a nephew of mine would force his wife to perform such a menial job. I thought I'd raised him to be a gentleman."

Still smiling, I answered, "A gentler man doesn't exist, Uncle Larry. You raised a wonderful man when you raised Bruce. Occasionally, though, the Lord has plans for His people which supersede old-fashioned chivalry. I'm not waiting tables for a career, Uncle Larry — just until Bruce gets through medical school. Then I'm going to have a baby every year for six years straight."

He looked alarmed. "Don't you think that's a bit much?"

"I don't know. I haven't had one yet."

He smiled, looking more like his old self. The silence in the room grew, as if we had nothing else to discuss.

"You want to know about Bruce," I offered. "He's working hard, and is an excellent student. I guess he really did know what he could do best. College subjects half bored him, but he really enjoys the challenge of med school. He earned a fellowship to help his tuition, and if he keeps up his good grades, he'll probably be able to get one every semester. He hasn't changed a great deal since our marriage, but he's learned to relax and laugh a little more. We're both active in the church you attended with us last Easter. Bruce sings in the male quartet and I teach Sunday school. We haven't a spare nickel, but we're supremely happy, and we wish you could be, too."

For a moment, a wistful expression flickered in the old man's blue eyes, now growing pale with age. He stared past me, at the wood paneling of his luxurious office. This man, who possessed every material comfort to the saturation point, still lacked one thing.

"Happiness, like truth, is an elusive thing," he replied slowly. "When you grow older, Sandy, you'll understand better. I envy you your state of mind, but tremble for you when you discover it's all a farce. Some day you will."

Like Adelbert, he was a prophet of philosophical doom. I never could understand their joy in being miserable.

Suddenly Mr. King came around his desk to take my left

hand. He turned the ring back and forth to catch the glints of the diamond.

"This stone has been in our family for four generations," he mused. "I'm glad you're wearing it."

Though the thought had never passed through my head before, I said, "I'm proud to be able to."

"Would you like to let me take it to the jeweler to check the points and have it cleaned?" he offered.

I hesitated. "No, I think it's okay. I soak it in ammonia every now and then to clean it. That works fine."

He did not press the point. We talked a little longer of a book we had both read, and I suddenly started to my feet. "It's getting dark, Uncle Larry. If I'm not there when Bruce arrives, he's all set to scour the streets for me."

Mr. King escorted me to the door. "I hope you've acquired some common sense in the last year," he remarked, alluding to the time I had wandered into Sheldon's Negro ghetto in search of my college friend, Mary Weaver.

"Is Joe Barrows still working here?" I asked. Joe was Mary's husband, and on my plea, had been given a job in the store by Mr. King.

Uncle Larry shrugged. "I haven't the faintest idea. Stock boy, wasn't he?"

Again, the hint of disdain for lowly employment. It soured our farewell. I had been on the point of inviting Mr. King to Sunday dinner. The sudden vision of this elegant gentleman entering our slum apartment gave me the shivers.

"Yes. I'll have to go see Mary some day. I never quite recovered the courage after that first excursion."

He chuckled. "Come again, Sandra. I love to see you. I believe Tom is waiting in the outer office. He'll drive you home."

We said good-by, and I went to waken Tom, who snoozed quietly behind a newspaper on a bench in the outer office. The visit had left me feeling vaguely anticlimactic. I'm not sure what I expected, but something a trifle more dramatic than an exchange of polite news. But then, the Kings were much too civilized to be dramatic except under dire stress.

Tom did not know where Prospect Street was. When I told him, he displayed a disturbed countenance. "That's not a very good neighborhood, is it, Miss Sandra?"

"My mother wouldn't think so," I agreed. "But we're not trying to impress anyone. The rent is low and the house is warm.

When we get there, come on in. Bruce may be home, and you'll see we aren't too bad off."

When we entered the tenement, however, our upstairs neighbor was sprawled drunkenly in the hall at the foot of the steps. His wife never assisted him — she always let him sleep it off wherever he fell. Tom did not consider this proper conduct, so between us, we hoisted the man to his feet and struggled him up the stairs. On our floor, Bruce opened the door to peer out.

"What on earth?" he asked. "Sandy — Tom! What are you doing with——? Here, I'll take him up."

He came and took my side. Bruce was big and Tom was small. When Mr. Davenport's arm were flung across both their shoulders, he looked as if he were sideways on a seesaw. I followed along, explaining my lateness to Bruce as we went. Both men were so out of breath with their load, they could only grunt.

They knocked on the Davenport's apartment door, directly above ours. A shuffling sound came from within. Finally Mrs. Davenport unlatched the burglar guard and let Bruce and Tom deposit her husband on the couch. I glanced in to behold the filthiest mess imaginable! Dirty dishes stood on the table, in the sink, on the cupboard. Curls of dust lay along the floor, and great splashes of dried food, as if someone had long ago thrown garbage at someone else and missed, dribbled down the wall.

The men strode out of the room considerably faster than they went in. I thought of my assurances to Tom that "our neighborhood wasn't bad at all," and could barely control my giggles.

"You have an amazing sense of humor!" Bruce snapped in irritation. "What's so funny about a couple of drunken sots?"

"Nothing. They're tragic. But I just got through telling Tom how much we liked our place. Oh, Tom, please come in and see— *we* don't live like that!"

"I'm sure you don't, Miss, but it hurts me to think of you living near people like that."

He followed us into our apartment to look around, just to make sure we were safe from the rough world. He turned to Bruce with a reproving frown.

"Bruce, you don't leave your wife alone in this house, do you?"

"Not any more than I have to," Bruce answered uncertainly, but I could see a worry beginning to formulate. "I've never seen the old man so drunk before."

I bustled into the alcove which served as kitchen. "He's no

menace to my safety!" I declared. "We like it here — the place is full of interesting people."

Tom turned to Bruce, his cap revolving in his hands. Awkwardly, in considerable embarrassment, he suggested, "Bruce, let me help you find a better place. Ellen and me — we don't have any children of our own. We don't use all the money we earn."

"Thanks, Tom. We'll make it on our own," Bruce replied firmly. I was very proud of him.

Tom didn't stay long. He had to get back to the department store to drive Mr. King home. Since the old man's recent illness, he did not drive himself.

Bruce listened with intense interest to everything I told him about his uncle. How did he look? Move around? Had he had a stroke, a heart attack, or what? Did he retain his old vigor? But when, as an afterthought, I told him about Mr. King's offer to have my engagement ring checked, a cloud shadowed Bruce's face.

"That's why he invited you to his office, then," he said slowly. "He wants it back. He doesn't want us to have even that tie with the family."

"Oh, Bruce, don't be silly!" I protested. "I think he just wanted to do something for us, without actually helping us financially."

An expression exactly like his uncle's appeared in Bruce's eyes for a moment. "Yes, Miss Innocent," he said. "Let's hope so. But don't give him any diamonds to clean."

We didn't know exactly what to expect from the afternoon's events. If Tom had walked in with the key to a clean apartment in a middle-class neighborhood, I would not have been greatly surprised.

A little, beat-up Ford sat before our entrance the next day as I returned from work. I started to go in, but was stopped by Tom's call.

"Oh, Miss Sandra."

Ellen was with him, her grim face breaking into an unaccustomed smile.

"Ellen! How good to see you! Do come in!"

Frantically I tried to remember the condition of the apartment. Ellen's meticulous housekeeping would put even my mother to shame, and with a "thing-dropper" like Bruce in the house, even a tidy room could become cluttered in a three-minute span.

While I held the door for them, Tom and Ellen reached into

the back of their car for some packages which they proceeded to carry into our gloomy building.

Because I was obviously expected to, I asked, "What's that?"

"Some things you left behind last year, Miss," said Ellen, in one of the longest speeches of her career. "You shouldn't have left those nice clothes all hanging in the closet like that. No one else could wear them. So I just packed them away in moth balls till we saw you again."

"Ellen!" I protested. "You shouldn't have! I didn't want——"

But why go into a lengthy explanation of old, buried hurts? The clothing had been supplied for me the preceding Easter when the elegant Kings found mine too shabby for their tastes. The sting of angered humiliation had never quite left me. When Bruce and I departed from the old mansion, I took only my own things, leaving the charity behind.

I unlocked the apartment door (no Mr. Davenport in the hallway this time) and held it open for Tom and Ellen, who dumped the boxes on the couch, then looked for a place to sit. Except for the three straight chairs at the table, there was none.

Through Ellen's exacting eyes, I saw our apartment as it must appear — shabby and barren — and our situation as she must see it — silly, chin-in-the-air "kid" stuff.

"I think the couch is the only comfortable place to sit," I said. "Why don't you put the boxes on the floor and I'll make some tea?"

It was very strange, entertaining Tom and Ellen in my home. As servants in the King household, they kept their unobtrusive place. Here, they were supposed to be friends, but I couldn't think of a thing to say to them. I found myself prattling about the weather while they sat and watched me scurry about the kitchen. Perhaps they felt as awkward as I.

It must have been an answer to unuttered prayer, for Bruce came home from class an hour earlier than usual. As he kissed Ellen's wrinkled cheek and shook hands with Tom, his shoe touched one of the boxes they had brought.

"You been shopping?" he asked in surprise, for we had just been lamenting the stringency of our budget.

"No," Ellen answered. "Your wife left some clothes in the closet last spring. I thought I'd bring them to her."

Bruce's right eyebrow arched. "Oh? I didn't know she had any spare clothes to leave."

He was more curious than I. I wanted to ignore them, perhaps just put them away in a trunk where I needn't be reminded of that week, but Bruce opened the boxes and drew out all the lovely, feminine things I could never afford.

"I don't remember seeing you in these things," he said. "Why don't you throw out your old clothes? They're getting pretty worn."

I would have been aware of his sensitiveness, but he was not to mine. I poured the tea, allowing that to serve as sufficient interlude to divert the answer expected of me.

Tom and Ellen did not stay long. They had come to see "their boy" and now that they had seen him, they were satisfied. With hearty good-bys and an urgent "do come again" we saw them to the door. Bruce walked to the car with them while I cleared away the tea things and sought a place for the clothes. He came in as I opened the lid of a trunk.

"What are you doing?" he asked.

"Putting these away."

"No, you're not. You need clothes, and the Lord is providing them. No silly pride is going to keep you from accepting His gift."

I was on the verge of tears. "Since when have your uncle and the Lord been synonymous?"

He put his arms around me. "Now who's being silly? If you don't want me to be suspicious of Uncle Larry, then you'd better not be, either. Be glad of one thing, Sandy — they didn't have the key to some apartment they wanted us to rent."

I hugged him. "Oh, did you think of that, too? It was the first thing that flashed through my mind."

"Great minds——" He dropped his arm from my waist. "I don't know about you, but that tea wasn't enough for me. What's for dinner?"

"Hamburger or tuna fish. Which would you prefer, sir?"

"With a menu like that, I'll leave the choice to you."

CHAPTER TEN

Adelbert Coogan sat on the top step of our landing one afternoon in mid-April, a letter in his hand. As soon as he saw me come in, he got to his feet. If his joints had not been well-oiled, I'm sure he would have clanked, for he moved like the Tin Soldier of Oz — each limb a separate entity, connected only by accident.

He'd had a haircut — the first in months. *And* he wore a clean shirt.

In spite of his non-conformity, Del had never summoned courage to call me by my first name. I had invented his nickname for him, for Adelbert seemed such a mouthful every time I wished to use it. We saw each other at least once a week, sometimes for a few minutes, sometimes for forty-five. Always he brought Tamara with him, in deference to Bruce's frowning disapproval. Probably because neither of them were "my type," I found them stimulating company. Our discussions, lively and heated, harked back to the days in the *Beacon* office, when we would argue for the mere joy of arguing. By the time Adelbert and Tam had visited me for the third time, I began to suspect Del didn't really believe the nonsense he propounded so much as he was exercising his freedom to be radical.

"Well, Mrs. King," he beamed as I came abreast of him, "I took your advice."

I blinked and stared. "You became a Christian?"

"No!" he groaned in disappointment. I fished my key from my purse and glanced at him. He was on the verge of bursting.

"Your other advice. You told me I should become an actor. Well, now I am one."

"Now you am one what?"

"An actor! A comedian! I have a job! You know the *Evening Star?* Oh, you wouldn't. It's a nightclub in the Crestview section. Beginning next week, I'm to be their sensational new comedian!"

He followed me inside. Tam was not there, but neither of us really missed her. I grinned and laid my things on the table.

"I never knew a night club performer before," I said. "Are they going to pay you for this, or are you doing it for the love of the arts?"

All Del's arguments against filthy lucre flew out the window. He forgot he'd ever had them. "One hundred and twenty-five dollars a week! I'm moving out of this dump next Saturday."

"Oh, Del!" I cried with a pang. "You're my only source of entertainment! I'll die of boredom without you!"

With a perceptiveness I didn't know he possessed, he replied, "Hah! You never give me a second thought! The minute that big hulk comes through the door, you forget anyone else exists." I grinned and picked up the broom. I could sweep under Del's feet without his even knowing it.

"Adelbert, when I first met you, I thought you hadn't a brain in your head. If you keep up, you may become a philosopher of sorts."

He inclined his head in what was meant to be a gracious bow, but turned out to be a quick jerk. "Your compliments are so pure, I think I'd just as soon have an insult. Will you come to see my act? Bring your husband — he won't like it, but——" his voice trailed off, and I realized he hated to say good-by.

I held out my hand. "Well, if it isn't slumming, Del, come back and see us. I doubt if we'd go to a night club, but we'll be——" I almost said "praying for you" when I realized the two didn't go together — "wishing you the best."

"Thanks." He shuffled to the door in his funny, loose-limbed way. "If I don't see you again, good-by, Mrs. King. Your husband really has it made, but I doubt if he knows it."

Without further lingering, he departed. It was the last I saw of Adelbert Coogan, poet, philosopher, and comedian, for many months.

As I hurried home from the restaurant one afternoon, I saw a short figure bearing a close resemblance to a walking tent dash out from our doorway and cross the street. The quick little steps were familiar; with a start, I remembered. I couldn't let the little soul wander home without a cup of tea.

"Mrs. Rosequist," I called across the intervening distance, "were you coming to see me?"

The tiny lady turned, her face lighting up like a child's at Christmas.

"Oh, there you are!" she twittered, waving her shabby old bag with the strips of carpeting sewn together. "I did so want to see you again, and this is the first I could get away. You know, they watch me so carefully, and——"

She took a step off the sidewalk. Intent on our greetings, neither of us saw the low-slung sports car as it slipped around the corner.

There wasn't a sound. The scene was caught in a giant still photo. A painter poised with his brush on his staging, a mother bending over her small child's stroller, Mrs. Ajarian rearranging her window display, the traffic on the corner — all froze in a stupefied silence. As soundlessly as a leaf fluttering from its branch, Mrs. Rosequist sank to the pavement, her tiny body shrivelled into a heap.

The quiet was shattered by the slam of a car door.

"Oh no, I've killed her!" a distraught matron, near hysteria, screamed.

Not even realizing I had run across the street, I knelt beside the emaciated figure, stroking her marshmallow soft hand. Tears dropped from my cheeks onto the little old lady's mottled skin. Not a drop of blood, not a bruise was visible. Fragile as a spider's web, Mrs. Rosequist's life had wisped out with the merest touch. She had not been run over. She had walked into the side of the car.

Her eyes were open in a vacant stare, and she was smiling. Still twitching, her lips gave out no sound. Before the rush of police and ambulance arrived, they had stopped moving.

A kindly masculine voice assured me, "You can't help her now, Miss."

"I killed her! I killed her!" the lady driver repeated, still in frenzied shock. I understood. I felt I had had a part.

Someone picked up the battered carpet bag to look for identification. Knowing the pandemonium which would follow if the wads of green bills were still there, I reached for the bag, keeping it tightly closed. No one questioned my right to it.

The police arrived, and then the ambulance. No one seemed to know the old lady. I answered their questions. The body was covered with a gray hospital blanket and placed in the back of the ambulance.

"Do you — shall I — go with her?" I asked.

The policeman shook his head. "She's dead, Mrs. King. You can't do anything for her. We'll get in touch with her family. Thank you for your cooperation."

He touched his hat and turned to the sports car driver.

Bruce was at my elbow then. I hadn't seen him come up, but he was there. Suddenly my knees gave out on me. He half carried me through the dwindling crowd, across the street, and up the stairs to our own apartment.

"She was coming to see me, Bruce!" I sobbed. "If I hadn't called to her — she was like a little child — she never looked at all!"

He laid me on the bed and stroked my hair back from my face. "I know, dear. But it was a good way to die. She had a smile on her face. And she knew someone was glad to see her. Maybe it had been a long time since anyone had welcomed her."

He always had the right words at the right time. But for many days my heart carried an open wound.

We visited the body at the funeral home, where it lay in unfamiliar splendor. Soft organ music piped in an eerie, mock-religious effect. She was not the Mrs. Rosequist we had met at all. Her fingernails were clean, and her lips and cheeks had been painted. Mascara dripped on her lashes. Where her own hair had peeped out in sorry wisps of gray, now she wore a wig of pure white softness. Her bright, beady eyes, once so full of life and surprise, were closed. Dressed in a lovely gown of pale blue chiffon, she lay in white satin shaded by lavender lights. Neglected in life, in death she was tended with elegance.

A buxom woman of fifty with features so like Mrs. Rosequist's that I knew her to be the daughter approached us in curiosity. Her eyes, unlike her mother's, were hard and indifferent. She was dressed as if for a formal tea, in a dark green dress, with long ear rings and matching necklace. No hypocrite, she pretended no sorrow. Her cold eyes swept my simple skirt and blouse.

"Were you — one of the servants?" she asked, in a tone of slight condescension.

Bruce answered for me. "No. We were her friends."

She arched her pencilled brows and turned on her heel without another word.

We left the funeral parlor. Outside, I could not contain my heartbreak.

"Sandy, sweetheart, she was an old lady. She had to die sometime. Why do you grieve so?"

"Because there's no one else to grieve."

Several weeks later, I read in the paper that Mrs. Nathaniel Rosequist (née Celia Burman) had left her entire eight million dollar estate to charity. Her daughter was contesting the will.

CHAPTER ELEVEN

Troubles never come singly. While we were concerned about Adelbert, Tamara and Mrs. Rosequist, there remained the major concern with Pat. She continued to attend church every Sunday, and seemed perfectly capable of coping with the babies during the Sunday school hour. Almost every Monday afternoon she came to spend a few hours with me. Though we studied the Bible together, I often felt we were not making much spiritual progress. She never seemed to experience the "joy of the Lord." Life continued to perplex her. Perhaps, without her husband's backing, she was afraid to commit herself to Christ. What knowledge she acquired seemed more head knowledge than heart knowledge. She only mentioned Don in passing now. Communication between them was dying out. I could not bear to pry.

Then one afternoon she was at the apartment as I returned with a load of groceries. Her face was a pale blank sheet, the pupils in her violet eyes widely dilated. Before she could open her mouth, I realized *she knows*.

It made no sense to pretend normalcy.

"I've left Don," she said bluntly, still too stunned to fully comprehend her own emotions. "He has a girl. Did you know?"

"I thought something might be wrong," I hedged. I set the groceries on the counter and turned to her.

"Why didn't you——" Pat stopped and began again. "Oh, never mind. I wouldn't, either. She came to the house, you know. I didn't even know who she was. I thought she was selling something. She said Don no longer loved me, if he ever had, and if I gave him his freedom, he'd let me have the house. She acted as if she owned him, and I was the intruder."

The words fell from her lips like water over a cascade of rocks. Once started, she could not stop. In detail she told how the girl looked, her mannerisms, her brassy laughter.

The terrible boil was bound to come to a head, but when it did, the pain was so sickening as to be unbelievable. I had no comfort to offer.

Pat had not allowed herself the luxury of tears. She paced up and down the room, nervously rearranging my sparse furnishings, completely unconscious of her dishevelled appearance. Her voice, always husky, had grown hoarse with suppressed anguish.

"And Don?" I finally asked. "What did he say?"

"It only happened this morning. I haven't seen him. I'm not going to."

"But Pat, if you give him a chance to explain – maybe he's not as involved as she implies. He must love you still. How could he choose *her* over *you?*"

She was quicker than I thought. "Have you seen them together?" she asked sharply. And I felt like a traitor.

"Once. They came into the restaurant. Of course, I couldn't be sure."

"I'm surprised Bruce didn't plow into Don."

"Bruce doesn't know. Pat, this thing is so sticky — please, can't we stop and pray?"

"I can't," she said. "God doesn't hear my prayers."

I put my arm around her and led her to the couch, where we sat, side by side. Then, while Pat stared blankly in front of her, I prayed aloud.

What could I say? The break-up of a marriage — two lives shattered — my voice broke, and I wept. Pat's veneer of composure cracked, then, and she dissolved into sobs so wracking they seemed near to convulsions. She was no longer talking, her sounds were mere babbling. I thought if anyone could have bungled more than I in the field of human relations, I would not care to meet him.

On this scene of female hysteria, Bruce entered. He blinked in the light, as if he could not quite believe what his eyes were beholding. Then he strode to the couch, where he lifted Pat's swollen face from the throw pillow.

"What's the matter?" he asked.

I answered, because she could not. "Don's been seeing another woman. Pat found out this morning."

"That rotten——" Bruce ground out the words and paused. "Pat, are you sure?"

She sat up, her body still shaking with sobs. "I'm positive. She came to the house this morning. She wants me to give him a divorce. She said it was a good thing we didn't have any children."

He asked the same question I had. "Oh? And where was Don during all this? Did he send her to do his dirty work?"

"I haven't seen him. I'm not going to."

Bruce put his arms about her for comfort, but perhaps his touch was too much like his brother's. Pat pulled away.

"Do you want me to?" Bruce asked.

"No. I want to drop out of his life as if I'd never existed. I haven't, for the last three months, anyway. I should have guessed — he was never home. All the old excuses — you know, and I believed every one of them. I thought he and Uncle Larry were getting along so well in the office that Uncle Larry was trusting him with extra responsibility. I'm a blind, stupid fool, and he played me to the hilt for it! I hate him!"

Almost anyone could threaten violence, but not the serene

Pat. Her lovely face had contorted with humiliated grief. Ugly red splotches dotted her clear skin. Bruce held her while she ranted.

I seemed unable to function. I stood in the middle of the floor, literally wringing my hands. Bruce glanced my way.

"Sandy, fix us something to eat, will you? We'll all feel better. Pat, stretch out on the couch till it's ready."

Like a little child, she said, "I need a drink of water."

"I'll get it," Bruce offered.

He went to the sink, filled a clean glass, and returned to Pat. She had been fishing in her purse, presumably for a handkerchief. Suddenly, Bruce gave a startled yell.

"Oh, no you don't!"

He slammed something out of Pat's hand, and half a dozen capsules flew across the floor.

"They're only aspirin," she said in a weak voice, as Bruce stooped to retrieve them.

"No, they're not. Where did you get them?"

"I haven't been sleeping well nights. Dr. Mahoney prescribed them for me." Pat was too exhausted to argue. She watched in resignation as Bruce went through her purse, dumped all the container's capsules into his hand, and strode into the bathroom, where he flushed them down the toilet.

The incident was typical of Pat. She lacked inner toughness. Rather than fight for her husband and home, she would run, or do away with herself. Even at that, the attempt had only been half-hearted.

I heated soup and fried bacon and eggs for a hurried meal. Pat barely touched her food, though she did make an effort to sit at the table. I marveled at her quick return to sanity. We tried to talk of other matters, but each subject proved a dead end. No one was listening to anyone else.

Finally, when Bruce had finished his coffee, he asked Pat, "What would you like me to do? Track down my brother and see what's going on?"

"No." About this, she was very positive. "Please, Bruce, give me some chance to salvage my pride. I haven't anything else left. Don't let Don know I came crying to you. I want to get away — out of this rotten city. Maybe — I don't know——" she affected a little laugh. "I thought of going out to California, but — I don't even know my mother's address."

What good would Pat's mother be to her? She didn't even

know which end was up, herself. On the spur of the moment, I suggested,

"Why not go to *my* mother's?"

A look of relief glimmered in Pat's teary eyes. Perhaps she had been secretly waiting for the suggestion. "Do you think — would she have me?"

"You know she would, Pat. Wait — I'll run down to the pay phone and call her."

Very providentially, I had received some extra tips on Saturday, or I wouldn't have been able to spare even the extra dollar and a half for a phone call home.

Of course, there was no question. Pat, or anyone else in trouble, was welcome to take refuge in the Marshall home. Mother was not curious about details. In her experience, she had heard it all, with one variation or another. She offered to drive up to Logan Airport to meet Pat's plane in the morning. Then, with a foresight uncommon to me, I called the Sheldon air terminal for schedules.

Pat had not brought a thing with her but her car and purse. She had walked out of the house without even speaking to the maid. She did have over a hundred dollars in her wallet — small change to Pat, carried around only for convenience. She had no plans for the future, but on this point she was adamant — she wanted no one to make an effort to contact Don.

Bruce argued himself hoarse, with no success. I was on Pat's side. Let Don worry a while — it would be good for his soul.

We were afraid to leave Pat alone. Bruce stretched his lanky form out on the couch while she and I shared the double bed in the bedroom. I meant to remain wakeful in case she needed help, but it was hopeless.

It was six when I awakened.

Pat's plane left at seven. Somehow, in the melée of three adults using the same bathroom and kitchen sink, I got them off. There was only time for a quick prayer before I left for work.

Spring sunshine made a mockery of human trouble. In a window box, bright jonquils poked yellow petals out to welcome the warmth. Forsythia bushes, unnoticed for eleven months of the year, blossomed in golden wealth against their drab background. My spirits lifted in the joy of breathing fresh air. And then I thought of Pat, and a lump of heaviness formed in my chest.

"What happened, honey?" asked the chef, a short stocky Italian with a wide grin. "You have a fight with your husband? You want me to beat him up?"

110

I smiled wanly. "Do I look that bad?"

"You look terrible. Believe me, you do. Here, have a cup of coffee on the house."

"Three more hours of sleep would be of more help."

But the day went smoothly enough. When necessary, it's possible to compartmentalize our thoughts; otherwise, we'd all go mad. I concentrated on French toast and pancakes for the next several hours.

Nothing happened. All day I watched for Don, or Tom, or even Mr. King. Surely someone would come looking for Pat? But no one did, not even at the apartment.

By one of Wednesday afternoon, the restaurant was crowded, with a few in the lobby, waiting for tables. I had just placed menus in the hands of six club ladies when a rough hand seized my shoulder and spun me around.

"Where is she?"

For half a second, I stared blankly at my brother-in-law. The fastidious Don King was close to wild in appearance. His white shirt lay open at the throat, his tie loose and to one side. With uncombed hair and flushed face, his breath fairly reeking of old liquor, he was almost beside himself.

From the corner of my eye, I saw the maître d' and the manager converging on us. They didn't care what happened to me, but please, no scenes in their restaurant!

"You're drunk!" I said to Don between clenched teeth. "Come into the kitchen and sober up!"

Before the two men reached us, I had pulled Don behind me, then literally shoved him through the swinging doors and into the kitchen. To my friend the Italian chef, I pled,

"Give him some hot coffee, and make him stay here, please."

With hardly a raised eyebrow, the chef poured coffee into a mug and set it on a cleared place directly before Don. I pulled up a stool for him, for he looked too tired to stand on his feet. His eyes were black from dissipation, or lack of sleep, or both, and his hands trembled on the mug handle.

"Don, I can't talk to you now. But stay put — don't get into trouble — and I'll come back. Okay?"

All this took less than a minute. I turned to meet the maître d' and the manager.

"He's in trouble," I explained. "Please leave him alone. I'll pay for his coffee."

With a contemptuous sneer on his foxy face, the maître d' asked, "He your husband?"

Indignation flushed my cheeks and I snapped, "Of course not!" before I realized he *was* my husband's brother.

Mr. Mylan took my arm to warn in a low, serious voice, "No more scenes like that, young lady. Keep your family troubles out of the restaurant."

"I'm sorry, sir," I said, and stopped. Kind as he had been to me, this really wasn't any of his business.

My club ladies cast furtive glances of curiosity as I took their orders. Such carryings on might shock the management, but they provided entertainment for the patrons, almost as good as a floor show.

The restaurant was nearly empty before I could get back to Don. He perched on the stool, his elbows on the counter, face to the wall, in such a spirit of dejection, a harder-hearted person than I could not have denied him sympathy.

I put my hand on his shoulder. "Pat's all right," I said. When he answered, his voice was sluggish.

"She's not in your apartment. I checked. The landlady gave me the key when she got scared I'd break the door down."

"How did you locate our apartment?"

"Tom and Ellen. They know everything."

"Does Uncle Larry?"

"I don't know. I haven't been to work for a couple of days."

Don's lids were half-closed. I was afraid he'd fall off the stool.

"They'll let me off work early, Don. Come on — I'll get my jacket."

I spoke to the maitre d' on my way out. Wednesdays were seldom rush days, and the only way he could penalize me was by docking my pay.

Don's car was in the parking lot behind Alphand's. His motions were so pokey in finding the keys that I offered to drive. Surprisingly, he let me.

"Where is Pat?" he asked, as I swung into traffic.

"She asked me not to tell you. You have some mess to straighten out before she'll come back, anyway."

He settled into a glum silence, paying no attention as I threaded my way through Sheldon's run-down streets. I parked in the lot down the street — just beside Pat's lovely cream-colored car, but if he noticed, he paid no attention.

With some of his old caustic tone, Don sized up our tenement. "What a crummy way to live," he remarked.

"Much crummier than the way you live?" I returned.

112

He snorted. As if in the habit of calling at our apartment often, Don stretched himself on the couch.

"Are you hungry?" I asked.

"I could use a drink, but I'm not apt to get one here," he said.

"No, you're not."

There was some left-over chili in the refrigerator. I heated and served it to Don, who ate without tasting. He was awaiting for his lecture, but none was forthcoming.

I set up my ironing board and left him to fidget until Bruce came home. He smoked one cigarette after another, barely allowing one to go out before he had lit up another. I wondered how long it would take to air out the apartment after his departure, for our living room windows were very small.

Bruce's welcome to his brother was hardly effusive. He stood inside the doorway, watching thoughtfully as he peeled off his jacket.

"Well, Don," he said at last. But he did not cross the room to shake hands with this brother whom he had not seen for ten months. The atmosphere immediately tensed. I took the ironed clothes into the bedroom and put them away. When I came out, the King men still faced each other without speaking, each waiting for the other to break the ice.

"Do you want supper now or later?" I asked.

"It doesn't matter," Bruce said. "I have quartet practice tonight, Don, so anything you have to say had better be hurried."

"All right," Don said, blurting out the words like a school boy. "I want my wife back. You know where she is. Tell me, and I'll go get her."

Not a hint of contrition in his voice — only belligerence. Don King wanted what was rightfully his, and he meant to have it.

"And what about your — uh — *friend?*" Bruce asked.

"Oh, that little fool! I'll ship her off in the morning. She had no business going to the house. I didn't even know Pat had left until Rose told me a lady with black hair had been there. Pat didn't even leave me a note!" He pondered his wife's injustice in an aggrieved tone.

"Perhaps she was rattled," I put in. "Most women aren't accustomed to having strange women demand their husbands in their own living rooms. As she gets more used to it, her manners will improve." Serious as the occasion might be, I never could resist giving Don a dig.

"Why don't you shut up?" growled Don.

I retired to the kitchen alcove to prepare the meal. There was a ham — I rather hated to waste it on Don, but it was the meat I had originally planned. I scrubbed sweet potatoes, placing them in the oven with the ham, while one ear was cocked for the men's conversation.

"What does Uncle Larry think of all this?" Bruce asked finally.

"He doesn't know, I hope. You—or Sandy—won't tell him?"

It was more a statement than a question. When neither of us made any pledge, he went on.

"If he found out, I'd be out on my ear faster than you were. To tell the truth, Bruce, I don't know how you stand this — slum. I couldn't live like this."

Always quick to bridle when someone ran down our apartment, I could have poked Don right in his self-satisfied middle.

Bruce replied, "No, we're not going to tell him. And we're not going to tell you where your wife is. I don't like your attitude, Don. Where did you learn your morals?"

"Well, get on with the sinner's sermon. I've been waiting for it."

"You came to us. We didn't come to you."

"All right. I haven't slept for several days. Look, I *have* to have Pat back by Friday. She knows why. Call her on the phone and let me apologize. And I promise I'll never do it again. There wasn't anything to that affair, you know. Lucy was just a girl at the office. Pat knows she's the only one I ever loved."

"I'm not sure you ever loved anyone but yourself," said Bruce harshly. "You're too glib, Don, and I'm not making anything easy for you. It's time for you to grow up and take on a man's responsibility. You're past sixteen, you're not a playboy, and you've hurt your wife beyond belief. Until we think there's evidence of real repentance on your part, we won't help you at all." Bruce looked into the kitchen. "Can I help with anything, Sandy?"

He would have liked to dismiss his brother, but couldn't quite bring himself to tell him to get out. Don, with all the King stubbornness, seemed determined to stand his ground until the desired information was obtained.

I set the table and the men seated themselves. Here was a paradox in Don — though he bitterly fought any form of religion, he bowed his head in respect when Bruce said grace in our home. In spite of Don's abominable behavior, there was a vestige of charm in the man.

114

By mutual consent, the brothers dropped the strain between them, and began to exchange news of the last few months. Instead of dwelling within the same city limits, they might have come from opposite ends of the pole. Don asked intelligent questions about Bruce's studies at the university, and in turn, told about work at the department store, and their mutual friends at the Club. They were two different worlds — one, struggling and penurious, but somehow, very challenging — the other, self-satisfied and moneyed, but not very interesting. I wondered if Don caught the contrast. He seemed to have forgotten momentarily the minor inconvenience of having lost a wife.

"You're a good cook, Sandy," Don remarked, in his first verbal exchange with me since he'd told me to shut up. "This is the first real meal I've eaten since Sunday."

If this was supposed to stir my heart with pity, it didn't. However, I managed an imitation of a gracious smile.

Bruce cleaned up after dinner, then put on his jacket, and handed Don's suit coat to him.

"I have to go to quartet practice, Don. You can give me a lift if you want."

"Naw. Take Pat's car. I'll just stay and keep your wife company," he replied.

"No, you won't. You think you can worm some information out of her by being nice, but you aren't going to. Out—now!"

Don, through the years, had learned to obey this certain note in his brother's voice. He put on his coat and reluctantly followed him.

Bruce wrote a letter to Pat that night, complete with his opinions on her future plans. He thought she should get a job in Bartlett and keep away from Don until he showed a little repentance. Considering the fact that this was the first letter Bruce had written in our married life, it was quite a voluminous epistle. He stepped naturally from a place of ignominy to the role of head of the family. Since Uncle Larry was to be excluded from this particular problem, no one questioned his right to the position.

Pat answered immediately. She loved Don and would come back if he would ask her. On the other hand, this was her first experience in a Christian home, and she *loved* the Marshalls, all of them. Mr. and Mrs. Marshall prayed with her several times a day, and she began to understand the comfort and wisdom of a loving God. Perhaps it was now that Pat first comprehended the enormity of God's gift to her. She evidenced more growth and spiritual perception in this one letter than she had in the preceding three months of Bible study with me. I used to feel I was speaking to her in a foreign language when I tried to explain the truths of God's Word. Now, at last, she experienced the inner peace of a child of God. Tears filled my eyes as I put down her letter. I even toyed with the idea of mailing it on to Don, then realized that perhaps it would be a betrayal of confidence.

In the same mail came also a letter from my mother. She was trying to teach Pat to cook and keep house, and found her a very apt pupil. Of all the people involved in this sordid affair, my mother was deriving the most enjoyment, for she missed her daughters, and was quick to appreciate Pat's sweetness in substitution. She was an excellent teacher. Until I grew up and away from home, I never realized how much I learned from her in simple conversations as we worked in the kitchen together. Now Pat, so deprived through all her childhood, was experiencing some of these same benefits.

What kind of explanation Don managed to his uncle we didn't know, for he came to our apartment no more.

Two weeks passed. Busy with our own activities, we pushed our deep concern for Don and Pat to the back of our minds. Then, one afternoon, Tom appeared in *Alphand's* with a written message for me,

> "Dear Sandra,
>   Please come to my office when you are finished
> at work. Tom will pick you up at three. Thank
> you.   L. J. King."

The stilted handwriting only accentuated the brusqueness of his summons. It never occurred to him that I might possibly have other plans, or not find it convenient to appear in his office at three. Furthermore, I considered it unfair to be the intermediary when family trouble arose. Mr. King and Tom both knew where Bruce was, and could have summoned him. I resented the imposition.

Of course, I went. Tom waited in the lobby for me again, but this time his congeniality was replaced by a more sober attitude. We discussed the weather and prospects for a good garden through the short trip to King's Department Store.

To add further irritation, Mr. King was "in conference" when I arrived at his office, and I was kept waiting for twenty minutes in the outer office. It was my laundry day, and a huge stack of dirty clothes lay at home, tied up in a sheet, waiting for a trip to the corner laundromat. I fidgeted impatiently, and was on the verge of leaving, when his hatchet-faced secretary nodded at me without breaking her frozen mask into a smile.

"Mr. King will see you now, Mrs. King," she said.

The old man watched me cross his big room with the heavy carpeting, a speculative expression in his pale eyes. They had been warm the other time; now they were frigid.

"Sit down, Sandra," he said, without further greeting.

I sat, but I said nothing, trying to keep my face a blank. Actually, I felt like a delinquent summoned to the principal's office for some unknown misdemeanor.

"What do you know about Don and Pat?" he asked bluntly.

"I haven't seen either of them for several weeks," I hedged.

"That isn't what I asked. You know they've separated."

"Yes. Pat came to me before she left town."

"Where is she?"

"She asked me not to tell."

"She's with your parents?"

I stood up. "Uncle Larry," I said, "what do you want of me? I'm not responsible for every trouble that arises in the King family. Don and Pat will have to iron out their own difficulties without benefit of my interference."

"I'm sure interference would be the farthest thing from your mind," he drawled bitterly. "Pat's gone along with you in your religion, hasn't she?"

"It's not *my* religion," I retorted. "I didn't invent it! It's orthodox Christianity. Pat came to *me* — I didn't seek her out. She needed help — spiritual help — because her own life was a void. You know that. You even used to make cracks about empty-headed women in her presence. Did you and Don think she was too stupid to understand? She's a lovely girl, sensitive, capable of a great deal more than she's been permitted to develop. If you say I've interfered, then school teachers 'interfere' with children because they teach them to read and write — parents 'interfere' because they teach them ethics — doctors 'interfere' because they recommend healthy practices. All I've done to interfere has been to point Pat to a loving heavenly Father."

"Oh, I'm certain of that," said he. "And even if this loving heavenly Father concept breaks up a marriage, it's all right with you fanatics?"

"Who told you it was breaking up a marriage? It *strengthens* marriages. Even as much as you hate our beliefs, you must admit that!"

"I admit nothing, except that ever since Bruce met that nut

in Korea, we've had nothing but turmoil in this family. A young man with his potential to waste himself on the filthy heathen——" he paused abruptly, surprised at his own vehemence. "Well, I've expressed myself on the subject before. That's beside the point. But when it comes to driving a wedge between a couple who were getting along well before – don't you think that's going a little far?"

"Is that what Don told you? That Pat's religion had driven a wedge between them?"

He was calm now. "Yes. He said ever since Pat began to attend your church she's withdrawn from him."

I stared at the pattern in the carpet, trying to think. "What reason did he give for her leaving him?"

"He says he doesn't know where she's gone. He thinks to some sort of spiritual retreat for prayer and meditation."

I waited for a second, reluctantly admiring the wiliness of Don's excuses. "And you believe that," I stated.

"Any reason why I shouldn't?"

"Any reason why you should? Have you ever seen Bruce or me or any of our church group withdraw for prayer and meditation without telling anyone first?"

"I pay very little attention to your church habits. But I suspect Don is lying. That's why I called you in."

Mr. King was a perceptive, intelligent man, and Don was a fool to try to deceive him.

"You thought you'd antagonize me into blurting out the truth. Is that it?"

His smile did not reach his eyes. With his hand he made a glowing gesture of admission. "Perhaps. What *is* the truth?"

"Why trust my word over your nephew's? He must live up to your every expectation with his non-Christian behavior."

"For a Christian, you're a very sassy young lady."

"I'm sorry. I don't mean to be. But I'm just not door mat material."

Now he did smile. "It's the only reason I like you, Sandra. You're not a door mat. Does Pat have a legitimate reason for leaving Don?"

"You could talk to her and find out."

"But you think she does." He had sobered instantly, and now his words came slowly. "If I know much about Christian beliefs, the only excuse for leaving a husband or wife is adultery. Has Don committed adultery?"

I shook my head. "I don't know."

"All right. Go along home. You didn't tell me a thing."

I pulled on my spring jacket and slipped swiftly across the room. As I reached the door, Mr. King's voice came softly,

"Come again, Sandy. I really like to see you."

Strange ways he had of demonstrating it!

"Good-by, Uncle Larry. I like you, too — even if we don't agree."

"Maybe *because* we don't agree?"

I blew him a kiss, and departed, all my strength drained. Don's days at L. J. King's appeared numbered, and I wished I could warn him.

On the spur of the moment, I turned down the corridor to his private office, what I hoped to see or say not clear in my mind.

A giddy giggle sounded from within the translucent door. I turned the handle and pushed.

The black-haired girl in tight skirt and satin blouse perched on the corner of Don's desk, her hand ruffling his hair. They stared, frozen, as I stood at the door. And all the grief I ever felt for Don evaporated.

I closed the door and turned back into the corridor.

I had more personal problems to worry me.

CHAPTER TWELVE

"Casting all your care upon him: for he careth for you." It was a verse I had learned in Sunday school many long years past. Over and over I said it, but I could not really believe it. Other cares . . . but not this one. My anguish was a secret, shameful thing.

Even now, I wish I could erase this out of my life. But it would not be honest. I did not trust God. I knew of a certainty that He had made a mistake.

All of our plans, all of our future, hinged on one important, unmentionable factor — that we had no children until Bruce had

119

completed his studies. Even with scholarships, we needed money to live, and I was the only one equipped to provide it. So determined was I to avoid even the desire for a baby that I kept away from young mothers all wrapped up in the tenderness of maternity.

For a week, I kept my suspicion to myself, praying it would not be so, not daring to suggest the possibility to Bruce for fear the thought voiced aloud would become fact. At work, I found it hard to smile. At home, it was an impossibility.

As he dressed for school one morning, Bruce cast me a puzzled glance. "Sandy, what's the matter? Do you think you're pregnant?"

The word was out, hanging in the air between us. And what should have been a joy shared became a seed of trouble.

I looked away, out of the dingy window at the gray, dirty wall across from us. "I don't know for sure. I hope not."

He sat on the bed beside me. "Well, you know, sweetheart, I don't really mind. I'd love to have a baby girl just like her mother."

"Oh, of course!" I cried, almost in tears. "But *not now!* We can't afford it! What will we do?"

He smiled. "I don't know. But if everyone waited till they could afford a baby, this planet would still be under-populated."

His attitude of calm acceptance angered me. "Oh, *stop* being so philosophical, and try being practical! What are we going to do?"

"With a baby? We'll love her and care for her and provide her with some brothers and sisters later on."

"Stop it!" I almost screamed. "We're not ordinary couples with an income! How *can* we have a baby? What about your schooling?"

He drew back, as if I'd slapped him. This big man with the craggy features and the sensitive mouth withdrew to some inner self with an expression I had not seen for many months.

"Aren't you even a little glad?" he asked. "Don't you want a baby?"

"Of *course* I want a baby! But not now!"

"Oh? When?"

"*You know.* After you've finished med school."

"That would be four years from now. Did you really plan to wait that long?"

Here again was a topic we had never gotten around to fully discussing.

120

"Where else would we find the money? Oh, Bruce, don't you understand?"

He bent to tie his shoes. "You'd better get dressed or you'll miss your bus."

"Don't you understand?" I cried.

He stood up, carefully not touching me. "Yes, dear, I understand. It will work out. I'm sorry you feel this way about it."

He started breakfast while I dressed. I wanted to explain, but Bruce's closed expression forbade the subject. I left without kissing him good-by.

Our closeness was gone. We were courteous, even affectionate, but the communication lines were out of order. Unwittingly, in my distress, I had touched on some tender nerve within Bruce. He said he understood my worry over finances, but he acted as if I had said I didn't want his baby.

I was ashamed. Ashamed that I could not trust the Lord to whom I pointed others, ashamed that my maternal instincts were so neatly buried. No thrill of expectation, no flush of undiluted joy filled my heart in that first month. What to other girls was precious delight became to me a burden I could neither discard nor accept.

I gave myself over to frenzied planning. I would work through the summer as waitress. After that, my condition would become too obvious for me to remain in public work, but perhaps I could become a salad girl until the last month or so. Bruce could attend summer school and first semester with a full schedule. Then — but who knew? Bruce said nothing, almost as if we had never discussed the subject. Daily, he asked me how I felt. Resentfully, I replied, "Fine."

Morning sickness, fainting spells, palpitating heart were not for me. They might have lent some distraction, some reality to the mess I was in.

Petty annoyances became mountains of aggravation. Bruce was accustomed to lingering over breakfast, after I had departed for work. When I returned in the late afternoon, more often than not, an uncleared table awaited my tired eyes. I didn't expect him to wash the dishes, but *why* couldn't he put his eggy plate to soak in the sink?

Where formerly I could smile at finding his laundry on the floor instead of in the hamper, now I only seethed with irritation. He did no manual work all day long — why couldn't he at least pick up his own dirty clothes?

But even as my mother had pampered my father, I had

pampered Bruce in the early months of our marriage. Cranky as I felt, I realized that now was not the time to institute a program of reform. I gritted my teeth and said nothing.

He was there, one Sunday, leaning against a tree at the fringe of the church parking lot, his suit coat rumpled, and his head sagged downward in a dejected, little-boy manner, as one scuffed shoe kicked at a stone, while the other caught it before it could be flung too far. Lost in my own trouble, I did not at first recognize him, but his brother did.

"Hello, Don," Bruce said easily, his hand outstretched. "Waiting for us?"

Don did not see the extended hand. He raised weary eyes to his brother's, and I knew he had been drinking. Drinking but not drunk.

"Yeah," he said. "I went to your apartment but you weren't there. Then I remembered it was Sunday. A good thing you still come to the same church." He jerked a thumb toward the rear of the parking lot.

"My car's over there."

Families in clusters of three and four milled past us, on their way to Sunday dinner. In his unpressed, expensive suit, Don seemed thoroughly out of place.

His breath smelled of whisky. I didn't want to sit next to him. I declined the front seat when Bruce held the door for me, and opened the back door, instead. Don raised an eyebrow, understanding fully my disdain for his company, but withholding his usual sarcasm.

He assumed he was welcome to dinner. His arrogance of the previous visit had vanished and he had no spirit left. A surge of sorrow for his plight stirred me, and then the vision of that black-haired secretary hugging his head to her, negated what kindliness seeped into my heart. My thoughts turned to lovely Pat, distraught with shock, sobbing in huge, wracking cries on the very spot he slouched now, and a bitter hardness quite foreign steeled me against any excuses or pleas he might extend.

The roast, in the oven since nine-thirty, was done. I turned on the potatoes and set the table. Then I went into the bedroom and closed the door, leaving the brothers to exchange whatever secret thoughts they might harbor. These King men tired me.

Twenty minutes later, when I came out to mash the potatoes, they seemed to have made no progress. Bruce was studying the adult Sunday school quarterly, and Don rifled through the pages of a men's quartet hymnal. I didn't want to be drawn into their troubles any longer, for I never seemed to do anyone any good. I wished Bruce would take his brother out for a long ride after dinner and leave me out of the entire discussion.

Don was hungry. We ate quietly, saying very little. In place of dessert, I placed some fresh fruit on the table. Don peeled an orange, divided it into sections, and left it untouched on his plate. Flatly he said,

"You know, I suppose, that I'm out? The old man didn't bother with a warning. Just get out, that's all."

Bruce's voice came quietly. "What warning did you need, Don? You know how keen Uncle Larry is, and how he feels about what you were doing."

"Who's *he* to be so pious? Do you mean to tell me — all these years——"

"Shut up, Don," Bruce said, his voice very taut. Whatever he thought of his uncle's harshness, he would permit no insinuations on his conduct. "You knew the rules. You broke them. Now don't scream when someone cries 'foul.' "

"Okay. I had it coming. Tell me what to do. I don't want to go crawling to the old man's friends for a job. I *hate* business, anyway."

"What *do* you like, besides wine, women and song?"

With a flicker of a grin, Don remarked, "Can't earn much of a living with any of them."

He leaned back in his chair, his hands jingling some loose change in his pockets. "A bit ironic, isn't it? Here I am, stuck with a seventy-thousand-dollar house, no wife to live in it, and no income to maintain it."

"He didn't take the house from you?"

Don looked surprised. "How could he? It's in my name."

"Why don't you sell it?"

"I'll try. But you might be interested to know there aren't long queues of customers lined up to buy seventy-thousand-dollar homes."

"Then get what you can out of it. Take the money, go back to college, and learn something useful."

"Like what? I'm not the studious type."

"Oh, Don, do you expect me to do all your thinking for you?"

"No. It isn't even what I came for." His coffee was cold now. He stirred it, not bothering to lift the cup to his lips. "I want my wife back. But I don't know how to ask her."

123

"She's working as file clerk in the school department in Bartlett."

"And living with the Marshalls?"

Bruce nodded without answering. Don fidgeted with the salt and pepper shakers, pouring a little of each onto the tablecloth, then moving the grains around with his fingers.

"What would they think of me, going up there after all this time?"

"I don't imagine you'll be received like a conquering hero. Why don't you stop worrying about yourself? You're the most self-centered person I know! You don't even want Pat because you love her, or because you're sorry you've hurt her! You want comfort because you've stubbed your toe!"

"Then why——"

"Because you're my brother, that's why! You make me mad, but I can't shake twenty-three years of looking after you. So I'll help you all I can, but I'd like to . . ."

He didn't finish. He looked chagrined at having so nearly lost control. Silently I applauded.

Don pushed back his chair to rise to his feet and glare sullenly at Bruce. His knuckles, pressed into a fist on the table, showed white.

"It so happens," he said slowly, "that I *do* love my wife. But when she got so religious, she just closed the door on me. She wouldn't loosen up and take a drink, she wanted to break away from the Club crowd, she'd have spent all her time reading the Bible if I hadn't put my foot down. Who can live with that? I don't want a harp-playing saint, I want a flesh and blood woman!"

"You did very well at finding one with real flesh and blood."

"That silly goose! It wasn't as bad as it looked, Bruce. I didn't intend to get involved with her. I still don't give two cents for her. She just happened along at the wrong moment."

Bruce banged the palm of his hand against his forehead in a gesture of disgust. "I know you're not a Christian, Don. But did you ever hear of moral fortitude? We're not characters in a modern play, who yield at the slightest provocation, then spend the rest of their lives snivelling at cruel Fate! You could have waited a few months for Pat to adjust. After all, she passed through a tremendous experience — from spiritual death to life. She knew nothing of true Christianity, and had to find out. If her appetite for the old life dropped off, it was because she was filling up on something better. Don, why don't you *try* it? If you accept

124

Christ as your Saviour, it will unite your family, give you some central shared interest."

"Not to mention saving my soul?"

"Yes, it will save your soul."

Don didn't sneer. For the first time in his life, he didn't sneer. He ambled across to the couch, where he sank, apparently deep in thought.

"Okay," he said. "I'll give it a try. No praying or big forgiveness scenes, but if Pat will come back to me, I'll go to church with her."

"There's no magic in church, Don," Bruce warned. "God deals personally with each individual. Unless you want a change in your life, God won't perform one in you."

"Why not? Isn't He all-powerful?"

"Yes. But He didn't create a bunch of puppets on a string. He created man with a power of choice. Each of us makes the choice."

The conversation had removed itself from my immediate vicinity. I finished clearing the table and ran hot water into the dishpan. There were a lot of dishes that day, for I hadn't taken time to wash the breakfast things before Sunday school. Don came into the tiny space which passed for a kitchen and picked up a dish towel.

"You know," he mused thoughtfully, "I wish you liked me. I've always wanted a kid sister, and you'd make a pretty good one. Just right for teasing. But not today. Today you look like the Great Stone Face. I didn't know they had female Great Stone Faces."

In spite of myself, I grinned. "Turn off the puppy dog charm, Don, and become a man. Besides, I *do* like you. I just don't find you very admirable, that's all."

He held a glass up to the light. "You left some milk in the bottom here. Did you know I was an expert on dishes? That was the big punishment for breaking the rules at Prep school. So I became quite an expert."

I had to laugh. After all the emotion-charged drama of the preceding half hour, Don's banter was disarming. He continued after a moment,

"Yes. I admit I'm not very admirable. Even I don't think so. I'm selfish and greedy and a real louse. But everyone has two sides to his nature. Did you know that? I learned it in chapel at prep school. Anyway, now that the bad side has been fully developed, maybe I'll start on the good side. Think I have anything to work with?"

I glanced around the cupboard at Bruce. He was pretending not to listen, but a grin had begun at the corner of his mouth.

"It's hard to say. If you work at it as hard as you have on the bad side, maybe by the time you're forty-six, you'll be half decent."

He groaned. "I'm dead beat, Sandy. Hurry up with those pans. I want to take a nap."

"Well, go. I can finish." I paused, to look him squarely in the eye. His eyes were red-rimmed and nearly drooping from lack of sleep. "Don, listen to me. When you go to Bartlett, don't act as if it had all been a gay lark. It isn't funny, not in the least."

"I know it. It's just a pose I adopt to get myself out of trouble. You know what they used to say about me in prep school? 'He's not a bad kid at heart, he's just mischievous.' Any other kid would have been expelled for the scrapes I was in. The head master and teachers felt sorry for me, because I was an orphan, so I slid by. And then there was always good old Bruce to bail me out if things got too bad. You see, I never stood alone, because I didn't have to."

His self-analysis startled me. I would never have been able to see myself so clearly.

While Bruce and I walked through the lovely spring sunshine, Don slept in our bedroom for the rest of the afternoon. Then, somewhat refreshed from sleep, he departed for Bartlett. At the door he paused to look back.

"In case I forget — thanks," he said.

"Good-by, Don, we'll pray for you," I promised.

He winked and closed the door after him. Bruce went down to the pay phone to call Pat.

Toward the end of the week, they were back. Hand in hand, they walked into our apartment, Pat's face more radiant than a young bride's.

Until they broached the subject themselves, we steered carefully away from any mention of the past. They had taken a second honeymoon trip through the Green Mountain range of Vermont, and returned thrilled with its quiet dignity. It might have been any couple dropping in for an evening, with not a hint of the nightmare of the previous months.

"We've decided to sell the house," Pat confided as she followed me out to the kitchen. "Don's awfully good at photography, you know. He wants to set up his own studio."

126

"Maybe he'll do better there than in the department store," I suggested.

Pat wrinkled her nose. "He hated working for his uncle. Sandy, I know this sounds queer. But it seems God allowed all of this, just to get Don where He could speak to him. He hasn't really accepted the Lord yet, but I know he will. Did you ever have the experience of knowing something before it happened? Your mother says it's 'assurance.' Your mother — oh, Sandy, she's the most wonderful person — and so is your father — they were such a help to me. You have no idea what a mess I was when I first went there. All I could do was cry. And then they would come and pray with me, and after a while, the most wonderful peace came into me. I never could have believed it! After a while, nothing mattered except knowing the Lord. Sandy, He's so real! Just like a Friend!"

To hide my tears, I scrambled through the silverware drawer in search of cake forks. Pat had reached a spiritual plane which was now beyond me. Once I had known Him as Friend. Now He seemed far distant.

Across the room, Don was laughing, his head tosssed back, his boyish face free of concern. He looked ten years younger than he had a month ago. But what went on in the mind behind the facade? How much genuine remorse did he feel? If I were in Pat's position, could I so easily enter into the spirit of forgiveness? I hoped never to find out.

In the weeks to follow, Don kept his promise. He attended church every Sunday morning, though how much attention he paid was impossible to assess. I feared for him. Everything was too easy. Whenever an obstacle crossed his path, he needed only to turn on his masculine charm to dissolve it. He could have an affair, and still bring back his wife whenever he decided to. He lost his place in one business, but still had enough money to set himself up in another. His outward show of religion would not deceive the Lord, but I was afraid it might lull Don into thinking he need never do anything more active in the realm of Christian acceptance.

The modern monstrosity they called a house was eventually sold — for considerably less than seventy thousand dollars, but enough to purchase a much smaller one, and still leave Don plenty for his photography investment. Of necessity, for they had neither the leisure nor the funds, they dropped away from the Club crowd. Don was eager, enthusiastic, dropping over often to discuss this or that with his brother. His years with Uncle Larry had not been entirely wasted, for, on his own, he developed a keen business sense for location and advertising.

"Everything would be perfect," Pat breathed to me in rapture one early summer evening, "if only I could become pregnant."

In embarrassment, I turned away. If she only guessed the turmoil in my mind at my own state, she would have been shocked to bitter disappointment. And so I kept my secret.

CHAPTER THIRTEEN

In every way, Bruce had been an understanding partner. He had helped me entertain Mrs. Rosequist without a demurral, though she would not have been his choice of company. He had tolerated Adelbert and Tamara's visits, though he considered them both a drain on the human race. He had dealt wisely with Don and Pat's problems. But on this one thing, my distress, he was completely without sympathy. An invisible wall of ice, it stood between us, never mentioned, but always there.

One Monday evening he announced that he had made an appointment for me the following Wednesday with Doctor Mahoney. I stood with my brush poised half way to my hair.

"Not so soon, Bruce," I said. "It's sort of a waste of time."

"The whole thing's a waste of time to you," he remarked acidly. "Mahoney is a good general doctor. If he thinks you need an obstetrician, he'll refer you to one."

He handed me the index card on which he had written the doctor's name and address. It was a good mile from *Alphand's,* in the opposite direction from Prospect Street. Too far to walk, not far enough to take a bus. I shoved the card into my purse, and, at the first possible occasion, called to cancel the appointment. Sometimes I could argue with Bruce, and sometimes I couldn't, but one thing I knew — no self-respecting woman went to a doctor before she was three months' pregnant.

128

Hoping the unexpected delicacy would divert Bruce's attention, I splurged and bought a steak for Wednesday evening. Quartet practice was at seven-thirty, which gave us only two hours together. Perhaps my conscious efforts to appear natural aroused his extra-sensory perception, for he finished his coffee, then pulled me close as I began to clear the table.

"What did Mahoney say?"

"About what?" I hedged.

"About the baby."

"He says it's a boy. Do you think you'll keep it, Bruce?"

Not in the mood for teasing, Bruce's arm tensed around my waist.

"Sandy, did you keep your appointment?"

"No. Bruce, I'll go next month. It's too soon — I'd be embarrassed."

"About what? You think if you ignore this business it will go away?"

"I'm not in delicate health! I don't need a doctor to tell me what I already know!"

We were quarreling again, almost as if no time had elapsed since that morning six weeks previous.

Bruce growled, "I'd like to turn you over my knee. Why don't you get some sense in your head? You're acting like a sulky child!"

I pulled away, to stand with my back at the sink. The faucet dripped an endless plink into the frying pan.

"Maybe I *feel* like a child! But I certainly don't get any comfort from you! You act as if everything's my fault!"

"What do you mean? *I'm* the one who's glad!"

"I *hate* hypocrites! You're just pretending, and you know it!"

I wanted to stalk past him into the bedroom and slam the door in a burst of melodrama. But the kitchen was too small, and Bruce standing by the table was hulk enough to fill the narrow passageway.

"*Hypocrite?*" he repeated. He reached for my shoulder and gave me an irritated shake. "Where's all this marvelous faith you urged me to exhibit last spring? 'Trust God, that's all we need to do,' " he mimicked. "*You* don't trust God. You trust yourself! As long as you have a job and everything goes *your* way, then you can 'trust God.' What's so trusting about that?"

I reached to release his fingers from my shoulder where they had continued to press.

"I don't know. But Bruce, if you'd only————" my voice

129

dropped. That familiar sense of shame enveloped me. I detested myself, but I didn't like my husband much better.

"Only what?" His voice was calm, and I knew at last we could talk.

I gave him a gentle shove. "It's crowded in here. Let's go in the living room."

He stepped aside for me to pass, then followed me to the couch, where he pulled me into his arms.

"Only what?" he repeated.

"*Sympathize!* Bruce, all the pinions have been knocked from under me, and you stand back and act — as if — I ought to be—some kind of stoic. I'm not! I don't know how we'll manage!"

"But, Sandy, *I'm* here! Do you think I'll let you starve?"

"I'm not worried about starving. How will we ever get to the mission field?"

He held me away to gaze in my face in bewilderment. "Do you remember, a year ago, when I asked you the same thing? You told me I was insulting God to doubt Him. If the Lord wants me to be a medical missionary, surely He'll take care of my preparation, Sandy."

"Oh, Bruce, that's easy to *say!* But do you really *feel* it?"

He answered slowly, "Yes, I really feel it. Why don't you?" He reached across me to the end table and picked up his Bible, leafing through until he came to Isaiah. "Here's a verse I found years ago, when I still lay in the hospital in Korea. 'Thou whom I have taken from the ends of the earth, and called thee from the chief men thereof, and said unto thee, Thou art my servant; I have chosen thee, and not cast thee away. Fear thou not, for I am with thee: be not dismayed; for I am thy God: I will strengthen thee; yea, I will help thee; yea, I will uphold thee with the right hand of my righteousness.' Sandy, what a beautiful promise! How can we doubt Him? We're going in His Name! He'll care for us!"

Like the slow opening of a door into a lighted room, I began to comprehend. The unexpectedness of my pregnancy was the least of Bruce's concerns. He had mentally placed me on some kind of spiritual pedestal, and I had tumbled off. Not my pregnancy, but my attitude, had stunned him. I wanted to cry. But weeping was one feminine trait with which Bruce could not cope. Saddened, I pondered several minutes.

He kissed me then, and the burden lifted as surely as if someone had literally removed a weight from my heart. We slipped to our knees in prayer.

Unlike New England, where spring and summer blend almost indiscernibly, Sheldon produced a heat wave with the first week of June. The sun beat on treeless Prospect Street with all the intensity of a tropical dry season. Heat shimmers rippled up from the macadam, and even the animals slunk into the tenement shadows with peculiar lethargy. The only ones unaffected by the sudden temperature rise were the children. It seemed our section of town was conducting a population explosion all its own. Bruce, never obviously enamored of the younger generation, now paused to chat with groups of boys, to show them how to swing a bat or pitch a ball. His limp, no handicap, made a further hero of him, for he had acquired it in a "real, live war."

His delight at the prospect of becoming a father was difficult to conceal. Paperback books, from *Childbirth Without Fear,* to *Baby and Child Care* mysteriously appeared on our bedroom dresser.

I don't like people to deal with me subtly. I think if they have something to say, they should come out and say it. And if Bruce wanted me to read those books, he should have said,

"Here's something you might be interested in, honey."

But of course, I read them — carefully placing them back on the dresser in the same place he had left them when I heard his footsteps on the stairway. It became a game with us. He knew, and I knew he knew, but neither of us mentioned these books to the other.

Bruce finished his first semester with honors. Through one of his fellow students, he acquired a job as substitute taxi driver for the two weeks between semesters. Since the streets of Sheldon were thoroughly familiar to him, he was delighted at last to have a share in the family earnings. When summer school began in mid-June, he was able to keep his job as part-time driver in the early mornings and evenings, often studying, then, till two in the morning. His energy seemed inexhaustible. In fact, he appeared more cheerful than I had ever seen him, and I realized how much it must have rankled with this proud man to rely on me for his support.

At the end of three months, entirely on my own, I made an appointment with Bruce's Dr. Mahoney. He was a youngish man, possibly in his late thirties, with a crop of crew-cut hair bristling like little porcupine quills all over his head. He smiled and shook hands with that preoccupied bustle associated with medical men.

"So you're Bruce's wife," he said as he sat himself behind his desk, to lean back in the swivel chair. "I saw him once on the campus a couple of months ago. How's he making out in school?"

"Fine. He does very well."

"Naturally. How's the rest of the family? Haven't seen any of them since Mr. King's illness last winter."

"Don has left the store," I said cautiously. "He's setting up a photography business of his own."

"Really?" Dr. Mahoney raised his eyebrows. "Then who will take over? It's been a family business for generations."

I shrugged. "The winds of change, you know. I imagine someone will want it."

He smiled. He had questions to ask, but he didn't know how far he dared go in personal matters. After hesitating, he asked,

"I understand Bruce and his uncle were estranged last year. Is that why I never met him at the hospital or the King home?"

"Yes," I said. "Uncle Larry didn't want Bruce to become a medical missionary, so he cut him off."

"With no money at all?"

I nodded.

"It's what I heard, but I didn't believe it. You know, my father was killed in an accident in King's Department Store just before I entered college. Mr. King put me through college and medical school. Those were the days before all this insurance business — so he didn't have to do it, but he did. Now when his own relative needs help, he won't give it."

I smiled. "We get along, Dr. Mahoney. Uncle Larry doesn't owe us a thing."

He cast an experienced eye over my expanding waistline. "But you aren't going to be able to work very long."

"We're not worried. The Lord will provide some other way."

Dr. Mahoney smiled. "Yes. Bruce became quite religious after his experience in Korea, didn't he? Well, you won't have any doctor bills, at least."

I flushed, grateful and embarrassed.

The examination proved what I had known all along, that I was a very healthy young woman.

Then, suddenly, unexpectedly, I was filled with a joy so exciting I could hardly contain myself. I wanted to tell everyone— we were expecting a baby! Boy or girl, blond or brunette, quiet or noisy, it was ours! A very special child!

But telling a stranger would have been easier than telling Pat, whom I loved so dearly. If it were a joy she shared, there would

132

have been only mutual delight. But her own lack of fertility ate into her like a physical deformity.

We were alone, on a hot summer afternoon in late July. All the afternoons that July were hot. When she heard my news, Pat's violet eyes brimmed with tears, and she searched for a handkerchief.

"Oh, Sandy, why you and not me? You can't afford a baby. It would be all I need to be certain I could hold Don."

The words were out before she realized she had voiced them. They shocked us both. Perhaps she would never again be sure of her husband. And in spite of our straitened circumstances, I knew I was far better off than she.

Don and Pat pretended enthusiasm over our good fortune. But they were jealous. It clouded our once-close relationship. A little chill of apprehension unsettled me. If we were to lose their friendship, after all these lonely months, it would indeed be a long, bleak winter ahead.

Of course, better than Bruce, I understood. I had hated listening to the "baby talk" of the other young wives in our church group. Fortunately, I had no interesting "symptoms" to discuss, and when we were with Don and Pat, we carefully avoided the subject. But still the thin separation existed. It showed mostly in Don's attitude toward me, for he was no longer rude. The banter had disappeared, as if I might now be so delicate my tongue would be incapacitated.

My waitress uniforms were becoming uncomfortably tight. I knew I would soon be forced out of the public eye. But the maître d' and I had never evidenced much appreciation of the other. I went to the manager to ask for a change.

"Salad girls don't make much money," he warned me, as if he thought I would alter my condition once I realized that.

"I know, but at least they make *something,* and I could stay off my feet most of the day."

"Okay," said Mr. Mylan. "Teach the salad girl to wait tables this week, and next week you can have her job."

Late that afternoon, Pat came to see me alone. In her hand she carried a package.

"Try it on, Sandy," she urged.

I opened the bag and pulled out a smart maternity outfit in soft yellow, my first and only.

"Pat, how thoughtful of you!" I cried.

"I thought it looked just right for you," she confided with

133

a shy smile. "Don't tell Uncle Larry, but it came from L. J. King's. I almost feel as if I'm sneaking in when I shop there now."

"Why don't you call on him, Pat? He's not mad at you."

She shrugged and shook her head. "I'm not comfortable with him. He thinks I'm a dunce. You're the only one he really likes. Why don't you go see him? Does he know you're expecting?"

"I haven't told him. If he wants to see us, he could invite us over. I wouldn't want him to think we were hoping for some handout now that the baby is coming."

She smiled confidingly. "Isn't this a tangled web? We'd all like to see him, and he must miss us, but no one wants to take the first step."

I was very sorry for Uncle Larry, sitting alone in his huge, dark dining room, with no lively voices to break his solitude. "If he weren't so *rich!* We could go and drag him out and make him forget his sulks, but now we think everything we do or say is open to suspicion because he might think we're after his money. Pat, I'm glad we're poor. At least we know our friends like us for ourselves alone."

Without realizing what had happened, we were back to our old footing. I went into the bedroom to try on my new outfit, and Pat opened some soft drinks she had brought. The color was perfect for my dark eyes and hair, but I could never imagine being big enough to fill out the entire growth allowance.

Pat half stumbled over her words, and I realized she must have been wondering all afternoon how best to word her question. "Sandy, after the baby comes, will you go back to work?"

"I'll have to. Maybe the experience will age me so I can get a job teaching. I really don't want to wait tables all my life. I think I've learned all there is to know about that particular employment."

She came out to the tiny kitchen, to lean against the counter while I worked. "Would you let me keep the baby for you while you work? I don't know anything about babies, but I could learn."

I looked up from my muffin tins, tears suddenly springing to my eyes. "Pat! Would you? Oh, that would be wonderful! Then we won't have to put her in a nursery. I always feel so sorry for these institutional babies. How could they possibly get enough love?"

Pat was smiling. She had moved a trifle to one side, and the afternoon sun cast a golden halo about her blonde head. No madonna had ever been so beautiful. "Boy or girl, it'll get lots of love at our house," she promised shyly.

I popped the muffins into the oven and pulled the potato salad from the refrigerator to season. Even with a cold meal, Bruce liked something hot.

For Pat, she was in a very talkative mood. What followed was almost a confession, delivered very slowly and deliberately. "Sandy, I think when we heard you were pregnant, we were both a little hurt because it hadn't happened to us first. You know, Don loves Bruce but he feels — not quite equal to him. He knows Bruce is smarter, and steadier, and clearer-headed. All his life he's been compared to him, and it makes him feel inferior. Anyway, when I told him you were going to have a baby, he looked almost hateful. He threw his tie on the dresser and growled, 'That so-and-so! He always gets ahead of me, even when he doesn't want to!' He wasn't very nice to me the rest of the night. I suppose he blames me because I just haven't been able to — Oh, Sandy, I've prayed and prayed. Why doesn't the Lord answer prayers like this?"

"He will, Pat. Just be patient."

"I'm trying. But it's hard. You don't know what it's like — to want something so bad, and month after month be disappointed. When they talk about too many children in the world, or legalized abortion, it makes me furious! I'd take *any* kind of child, crippled or blind, just a child of my own!"

"Could you adopt?"

"We'd have to be married five years before the adoption agency will consider us. Then we have to prove our married life is harmonious, and so on. We *will* adopt, if we have to, but we want our *own!* Is that so unreasonable?"

"No. But stop worrying, and leave it with the Lord."

Pat shook her head with an impatient frown. "You never get upset, do you? You accept everything in life calmly."

The pang of reproach! What would Pat think if she ever knew of my rebellion over this baby the Lord had given me? I could never tell her of my great sin, for she would never understand.

"No, I don't, Pat," I said honestly. "All I've learned is that the Lord knows best. He really does. We can plan and plan, and nothing turns out the way we think it will. But He has a master plan. This is all I know, and I have to keep reminding myself of it, because lots of times I really don't believe it. If you knew me the way I really am, you'd be ashamed of me."

135

Pat's eyes showed her disbelief. "Oh. Well, that isn't what I started out to say. I wanted to tell you about Don. At first, he sort of sulked — I don't know if you and Bruce noticed or not. Then, all of a sudden, last night he suggested I offer to keep your baby so you could work. In all the years I've known him, this is one of the few unselfish things he's ever done. I suppose it isn't completely unselfish, because he wants to be around the baby, too." She paused to laugh. "He even promised to come home for lunch to help me. But, Sandy — it's a start. At least he isn't going to let it be a strain on our relationship now. Your baby will have four parents instead of two."

"So now when she grows up and begins psychiatric analysis, she can blame four people instead of two for all her problems," I added.

Uncle Larry might consider Pat a dunce, but she was extremely perceptive where it counted most. She knew her husband, she cared for him, she was a perfect wife for him. Women with genius ratings could not have done so well.

Our baby was due at the end of January. But here, in the middle of August, we had her future all planned. At least, planned as well as humans can foresee.

CHAPTER FOURTEEN

At first I thought it was my imagination. Then it came again, gently, like the tentative flutter of a butterfly's wing. Our baby had moved! It was alive! I shook Bruce awake.

"Bruce! Feel it! The baby moved!"

"Where'd it move to?" he mumbled groggily.

I guided his hand to the proper spot. "Can't you feel?" I asked. "There it goes again."

He grunted, quite unenthusiastic.

"Aren't you happy?" I demanded.

136

"Sure. But I can be happy in the middle of the day as well as the middle of the night. Go back to sleep."

He turned over before the last word was out. But I lay awake for an hour, waiting to see if our child would move again. The thrill of knowing I carried a living human being within me was unbelievable. It was a miracle of such magnitude that I could hardly keep from telling others. But there was no one to tell. Mrs. Ajarian, the Davenports, the bus driver, the little Italian cook at *Alphand's?* Hardly appropriate. I kept quiet. But all day long I harbored a secret smile. Our baby was alive and growing.

When I left *Alphand's* at shortly after three that afternoon, the heat from the sidewalks slapped into my face like a scorching wave, shocking me. Everyone moved slowly, the people along the streets, even the traffic. It was the hottest day of an incredibly hot summer.

Ahead, at the next street corner, I saw my bus. But I could not force my languid feet to move fast enough to catch it. It pulled out as I came abreast of its rear door. The afternoon sun was vicious in its intensity. Even the metal lamp post was too hot to lean against.

The second time my name was called, I focused on the driver. His hair was neatly cut and combed, his face nearly clear of skin blemishes. He sat in an elegant white convertible with the top down.

"Hey, Mrs. King! Mrs. Sandy King! Over here! C'mon! I'll give you a ride home."

He was in the second lane of traffic. Behind him, auto horns had begun to honk, and some cars pulled around to pass. He was in danger of angering the whole east-bound population of Sheldon. I stepped off the curb and scooted in front of a car driving in the first lane.

"Adelbert Coogan!" I cried. "I never expected to see you here! How are you?"

He pushed open the car door on my side to reveal flashy red bucket seats. "Get in, Mrs. King, before a cop heads my way. I'm fine. How are you? Wearing the young marrieds' uniform, I see."

It was the first day I had worn the yellow maternity dress Pat had given me.

"Fasten your seat belt," he said. "We'll take a spin out in the country to cool off."

"Thanks, Del, but I'd better get home. Bruce comes in for

an early supper, then goes out to drive a taxi the rest of the evening."

"How's Tamara?"

"She got married a month ago — some guy from high school."

"Oh, I'm disappointed. I thought maybe you'd marry her."

He laughed like the little boy he was. "Slavery is not for me!" As if he were striking off the chains of imprisonment, he waved a fist in the air.

"Well, you seem to have been successful," I observed. "Are you still entertaining in night clubs?"

"Yes, sweet lady. I make a very handsome living with my dry wit and off-beat humor. It may be lucre, but it sure isn't filthy. You never caught my act, did you?" Those ridiculously long lashes swept his thick glasses like vertical windshield wipers.

"No, I'm sorry. I'd like to see you perform some day, but——"

"You couldn't afford the cover charge in one of those joints." He reached into his shirt pocket, and drew out two white slips of paper. "Here. With the compliments of the house. I don't expect your husband to like it, but you will."

I smiled. "Del, thanks. But night clubs just aren't our dish of tea. We just wouldn't have any free evenings, with Bruce driving a taxi now."

We were not heading in the right direction. I pointed this out to my chauffeur, but he only laughed in his innocent manner.

"Relax. You need the air. I solemnly promise to behave like a true gentleman."

We were out of the city limits now, streaking along the divided highway away from Sheldon. The wind whipped my hair straight behind like a mop in a hurricane. I wished he would slow down. I wanted to talk to him about more serious matters.

A sudden tooting on our left showed another late model convertible directly beside us, with a young man about Del's age at the wheel. With his index finger he pointed straight ahead, but he kept pace with Del's car.

"What's he want?" I shouted. "Why doesn't he pass?"

"He wants to drag. You game?"

"No! Please don't, Del!"

"Just up the hill, then I'll let him pull ahead." He hit his horn twice to indicate he was ready, and the cars sped along the white highway so fast the landscape blurred into a brown and green streak. They were equally matched, and the drivers were skillful. After Del's speedometer hit ninety-five, I tore my eyes away. With exhilaration taking the place of fear, I tried to sit back, to keep from shrieking. We crested the hill. And there, directly before us, moved a sluggish red tractor. It had pulled onto the road from a dirt path just a moment before.

Del tried to pull around it, but the other driver had not perceived our danger in time to give us room. We swung into the blue convertible with a nauseating clash of steel on steel. Adelbert Coogan emitted one loud "Ahh!" and was silent.

For what seemed minutes, the two cars carromed crazily across the road. My body felt as if it were torn from my legs. I screamed and screamed, but the wind caught the sound and carried it off. We jolted to a standstill, both cars a tangled havoc.

The quiet was an oasis. Strapped in my seat, I lay back and stared at white puffs suspended in blue. Nothing moved. I dared not look to my left, for I would begin to scream again. *There's blood on my new yellow dress,* I thought.

Then the sounds began. Car doors slammed. Brakes squealed to a halt. Voices spoke a jargon I could not interpret. Faces blurred in and out of my vision. Far off, in the distance, a siren wailed. The sun was very hot.

A man in a wide straw hat was asking questions. I tried to answer, but the power of speech had left. I drifted in and out of awareness. It was a long time before my seat belt was cut away and I was lifted out over the jammed door. On the ground lay two forms neatly wrapped in grey. I knew it was my last glimpse of Adelbert Coogan and his unknown companion in speed. But the numbness allowed for no grief.

The tunnel was long, and very dark. Gentle whispers, softer than the human voice, caressed my ears. I was floating, drawn by a fragile current, toward the light at the other end. I could not see the light. I only knew it was there. All was blissful peace.

From another sphere, an unfamiliar male voice intruded. "She's slipping away. I'm sorry, son."

Two hands clasped my cheeks. "Sandy, come back! I *need* you!"

Bruce was crying. His hot tears splashed on my cheeks. But I didn't want to come back. I wanted to continue drifting in that lovely, dark tunnel, toward the golden light at the other end.

He called again and again. My progress halted. I was floating no longer. The whispering had ceased. I opened my eyes.

"Let me go, Bruce," I pled inaudibly. My lips mouthed the words, for no sound issued.

"No!" he said, as my eyes closed again. "You must come back! I need you!"

It was a tug of war between two worlds, the known and the unknown, the pain-filled and the peaceful. I longed for the serenity my tunnel promised. But there was Bruce. Reluctantly, unwillingly, I turned back.

The room was full of color. Orange and brown and yellow, pale green, bright red and pink and beige. Blurring together in jumbled disarray, they formed no definite shape. A man was in the room. I could hear his voice, but I could not forcus on his face. Dimly aware that he had been with me off and on for a long time, I stirred my sluggish memory. An office. Why was I in his office? He bent over and pressed my eyelids open.

"Sandy, do you know me? I'm Doctor Mahoney. Try to stay awake for a few minutes, will you?"

With tremendous effort, I blinked my eyes open. Those were drapes at a wide window — beige with bright red and pink roses. This recognition seemed more strain than my mental processes could bear. I closed my eyes. The walls had been pale green. What was brown and orange and yellow? It seemed very important. I opened my eyes. Flowers—a spray of fall chrysanthemums in a wicker basket.

The man wanted to talk. Who was he? Doctor Mahoney, in an office, with a graying crewcut and horn-rimmed glasses. Oh, yes. My baby. I was going to have a baby. Could it be born so soon? The time had gone very fast.

"The baby——" I mouthed, though I could not hear my voice.

He took my left hand and came so close I could see nothing but his face.

"Sandy," he said slowly, his voice coming from a cardboard tube. "There was a bad accident. Your baby couldn't live."

The interior of my brain jogged to a sudden awareness, with a start of genuine physical pain. It all came back in an agonizing flash — the hurtling wreck, the deathly silence, the gray-wrapped bodies.

Our baby was dead. I had never held her in my arms nor felt her sweet breath on my cheek. She was dead. I had killed our baby. Would Bruce ever forgive me? I could not forgive myself. Our baby was dead.

140

I said it aloud, as if the words, once voiced, would no longer be true. "The baby is dead?"

Contradict me, Doctor Mahoney, please say it isn't so.

"Yes," he said. "I'm very sorry. But you can have others."

I wished he'd leave me alone. I turned my head and a dozen hammers pounded in my brain. The physical pain proved welcome relief to the mental anguish of a moment before.

Doctor Mahoney released my hand. "Bruce will be here in an hour. Try to rest until he comes."

Something was attached to my right arm. I couldn't move it. It hardly seemed worth the effort. I dozed, waking now and then to the realization that some dread ill had struck. Sometimes I knew what it was; sometimes I didn't. The ache was as steady and throbbing as one immense boil.

Bruce's face hovered anxiously over the bed from time to time. I couldn't talk to him. My mother was there, her strained face pretending a cheer she did not feel. She had grown quite gray in the last year. Did I do that, too, I wondered? Pat, in a soft lavender dress. Or white or blue. Once Don was with her. Dr. and Mrs. McPherson prayed on either side of the bed. I wished they would stop. God had turned His face from me.

It was His punishment. I hadn't wanted the baby at first, and He had taken her from me. A just God, but not a loving One. Once in a while, in my dreams, I stood just inside the dark tunnel, but the gentle voices whispered no longer. I was an intruder.

Night differed from day only in the blue lamp shining above my door, casting its eerie light over the shape of the furniture. Sometimes, the drawer pulls assumed eyes which peered accusingly at me, and my heart beat in inexplicable terror. *It's only a nightmare,* I told myself, *in the morning it will be only a chest of drawers.* On the edge of madness I hovered, fighting more fiercely for my sanity than for my life.

The day nurse was a buxom woman with frizzled red hair and splotchy brown freckles. She would have been more at home riding to hounds than masquerading in a nurse's costume. Apparently under the impression all seriously ill patients reverted to infancy, she employed baby talk when she wanted cooperation. She always irritated me; one morning, especially so.

"Does-um want some soup? Open your mouth for nursie. That-at's a good girl!"

"Stop that idiotic prattle!" I spat out. My head jangled with quick sharp pains, and I decided immediately to drop that tactic.

From the foot of the bed, Doctor Mahoney laughed aloud. I had not heard him enter the room. "You must be feeling better," he said, coming around to my left. "I haven't heard so much conversation from you in ages."

For the first time, my head was clear. "How long have I been here?"

"Ten days. You're coming along fine."

"When can I go home?"

He looked mildly astonished. "I don't know for sure. You've been rather banged up."

"Is Del——" I left the question hanging in the air.

He hesitated. "Both drivers were killed instantly. Your seat belt was all that saved you. And the prayers of your family and friends." The doctor was vaguely embarrassed. "I'm not a church-going man, but I know there are certain limits to medical power. You can be grateful for your religious faith."

Two tears edged their way out from under my eyelids to trickle onto the pillow. If he only knew how limited my faith was!

"Now, dearie, don't you cry. It'll only give you a headache," cooed the nurse as she wiped my face with a paper handkerchief.

"Uh — Miss Newton——" suggested Dr. Mahoney tactfully. "I think Mrs. King would like to be alone."

"But, Doctor, she hasn't finished her soup!"

"That's all right. It's probably cold, anyway."

He held the door for her until she bustled indignantly out. Then he laughed.

"We employ nurses like her so our patients will get better and go home. Does it hurt to talk?"

"Everything hurts."

"It will for a while. We're going to ease off on the dope now. We don't want to make an addict of you. If it gets too bad, let me know."

He picked up my left hand, turning the ring to catch its sparkle. "Sandy, I know this has been tough for you. But it's been even worse for Bruce. Try to keep things easy for him, will you?"

He didn't elaborate. I supposed he meant I was not to cry or bewail our fate. It seemed like a big order. And as time went on, it proved even bigger.

With a faith far greater than mine, Bruce registered for classes at the University. He never mentioned money. Just how, without my earnings, he would support himself, he did not say. I worried about him. He had lost nearly twenty pounds, and was obviously not getting enough sleep. His eyes were dark-rimmed and his limp became noticeably pronounced — a sure sign he was disturbed. But with me his manner was unfailingly gentle and tender. For an hour at a time, he would sit by my bed, holding my hand, saying very little.

"Bring your books and study," I suggested. "I just want you near me."

Even now, it was effort to talk, but there were certain things I had to say.

My mother was in Sheldon for three weeks, staying in Don and Pat's extra room. She spent an hour every afternoon with me. The rest of the time she occupied with teaching Pat to cook and sew and shop economically. I felt Pat knew her better than I did. But Pat had been deprived of a mother's guidance all through the years, and now she revelled in the delight of one good woman's attention.

One afternoon Mother brought in a picture of a new-born baby, a little dark blob with indistinguishable features. I was mystified.

"Your first nephew," Mother announced with a smile. "He was born the day before your accident."

I had temporarily forgotten. Ray seldom wrote. Ann never did.

"How's Ann?"

"Fine. A little nervous, but she'll make a good mother. I was in Texas when Bruce's call came for prayer."

My words still came thick and slow.

"Did I spoil things for them?"

"Nothing spoils the joy of a new baby, dear. You'll see."

Everything about my mother spelled hope and trust. But I couldn't believe her. I didn't believe I would ever want to smile again.

The next weekend my father drove down to take her back to Bartlett. They came in together to pray and wish me a final good-by. We had shared some precious times together, and now I thought I couldn't bear to see them leave. I had never been an apron-clinger, but now I wanted my parents near me. It was as hard for them as it was for me. But we Marshalls have always steeled ourselves against emotional defeat, and now it stood me in good stead. I didn't weep until they left the hospital.

143

Time refused to move. I could waken, thinking I had slept through an entire night, only to find it had been a half hour. A day often seemed to take longer than a week should. I could not hold a book to read. The TV on the wall jangled my nerves with its meaningless jargon. Even when turned off, its blank eye stared stupidly. Sounds in the hall left me feeling excluded, as if the world managed very well without me.

One afternoon Miss Newton wakened me from a fitful doze with the gushing information that "we must get ourselves all pretty because we have company coming."

She brushed my hair and washed my face, and that was the extent of my beautification process. Her mannerisms were now familiar to me, and she no longer grated on my sensibilities, for she was a genuinely concerned nurse. Every little improvement in my condition she cheered on like a pep leader at a football game.

"Now you can come in, Mr. King," she called coyly, and I wondered why Bruce's visit should excite Miss Newton so unduly.

It was not Bruce who entered. It was his Uncle Larry. He stood rather diffidently at the side of my bed, turning his hat in his hands. I gasped in momentary surprise, for, lost in my own troubles, I had forgottten his existence.

He bent and brushed his clipped mustache briefly against my cheek. "How are you, Sandra?"

"All right. I'm glad to see you, Uncle Larry."

"I'm glad you're awake. I've been in before, but you were too heavily drugged to recognize anyone."

"Oh. Did you meet my mother and father?"

"Pat introduced your mother to me. A lovely woman. I think you'll be like her."

"Not much." I flickered a smile, wondering why no one had mentioned this thaw in the old man's attitude. But of course, he was only theoretically estranged from his nephews, not their wives. Had he seen Bruce? The thought must have transferred to his mind, for he said,

"I haven't seen Bruce since the first week of your convalescence. How is he?"

"Working too hard. He looks sicker than I do."

I shouldn't have said that. Bruce would be very annoyed if he thought I had betrayed his fatigue to his uncle.

"He did register for classes then?"

"Yes. He's carrying a full load, and driving a taxi mornings and evenings besides. He studies while he's visiting me."

"He must have learned to organize his time better than when he was a boy." Uncle Larry smiled, the very picture of a gentle old grandfather musing over mellow reminiscences. He had brought me a book of verse, slender enough to hold in my left hand. We talked about current authors and a concert he had attended. He knew more about everything than I did, and his conversation was the most stimulating I had heard in weeks. I wished we could be better friends.

He had pulled up a chair. When I began to tire, he rose abruptly, prepared to leave. "Sandra, I've been talking to Bob Mahoney. He feels you could be released from the hospital next week if you had adequate care in the home." He shifted his hat from one hand to the other. "If you and Bruce wish to consider it, my home is open. Don't give me an answer now. Talk it over with Bruce, and let me know."

He bent and kissed me lightly on the cheek once more. "Good-by, my dear. Sleep well."

The overture on Mr. King's part almost overwhelmed me. He was willing to take Bruce back in his home! More than appreciation for the haven offered, I was grateful for the opportunity to declare a truce. But pride died hard with these Kings, and Bruce would not react well to accepting his uncle's charity. As naturally as breathing, I began to pray. I drifted off to sleep. When I awakened, hours later, I realized it was the first prayer I had uttered since the accident. A sense of well-being permeated the room. I knew the Lord had been there.

Like an old, forgotten hymn, these words sprang to mind: "And we know that all things work together for good to them that love God, to them who are the called according to His purpose."

The dreariness which had pressed on all sides suddenly lifted. Where had I been to fail to behold the loving care of a God who had preserved me even through the valley of the shadow of death?

If I could only wait on the Lord to make all things right. But impetuosity was more my attribute than patience.

Bruce's limp sounded a good ten feet from my doorway. When he entered, his face revealed exhaustion. But he brightened and came forward with a quick smile.

"Sweetheart, you look good. Are you feeling better?"

"Much. I don't know what was the matter with me. All of a sudden, I'm glad to be alive."

"I'm glad you're alive, too."

"Did you know, Dr. Mahoney said I could go home next week?"

Bruce's expression was unbelieving. "He didn't tell me that, and I talked to him yesterday."

"He didn't tell me, either. He told Uncle Larry."

The smile froze on Bruce's face. "Uncle Larry? What——"

"Bruce, please." I shifted in bed to draw closer to him. A sharp pain in my shoulder reminded me my bones were not altogether knit. "Uncle Larry came to see me this afternoon. He was very nice — like a benevolent grandfather. We talked about books and music and — it was like old times. Then, just as he was leaving, he asked if we would both come home till I was better."

"What did you tell him?"

"I didn't say anything. He told me to talk it over with you."

"He could have asked me first."

"Please, Bruce, don't be sticky. You know this was quite a concession. It must have been hard for him to say that much."

Bruce replied exactly as I had feared he would. "We're getting along fine. We don't need his help."

I turned away to hide my disappointment. "Maybe he needs ours."

He snorted. "Huh! Uncle Larry never needed a thing in his life."

"He never *admitted* he needed a thing. But he needs love and companionship, Bruce, just as much as we do. We're the Christians. We could give it to him."

He shifted unhappily. "Let me think about it a while."

"It would be better if you'd *pray* about it."

"All right. I'll pray about it. I don't really want to, though. If we go back to that house, it will be in the form of poor relatives.

146

Everything will be a handout. He'll knot the web so tight we'll find it hard to break loose again."

"Bruce! Your uncle isn't malicious!"

"No. He's a tyrant. I lived under his roof for twenty-two years. You were there only one week."

The bitterness rankled still. The wound to Bruce had been deep, but he was making the mistake of keeping it perpetually festered.

"All right, dear," I answered, suddenly too tired to think. But Bruce didn't open his books. He had already made his decision; now he was searching for reasons to justify it.

"It would make it hard for Don, too," Bruce went on. "If I were welcome in that house, and he wasn't, then he might think I was trying to get something denied him. Ever since we were kids, he's been scared I'd be one up on him — and half the time I was!"

It occurred to me he wasn't giving Don much credit for nobility. I closed my eyes, confused. Granted, Uncle Larry was a hard man, but he had never struck me as a devious one. Nor did I believe he was interested in dividing his nephews.

Perhaps he did show only his good side to me. He had made the first move in cracking the barrier thrown between his family and him. If we refused the next move, it would be shut tighter than ever. This was not good for either Bruce or Don. Grown men they were, but not yet grown beyond the need for an older man's advice. They valued their independence. Family spirit could combine with independence at no geninue loss and much real gain.

Through the next day I worried over the problem, mulling each facet with my limited understanding. Neither well nor wise enough to arrive at any conclusion, I was forced to leave it with the Lord.

Bruce came to visit in the evening with a slightly mellower attitude. "Sweetheart, I wasn't thinking of you. You're anxious to get out of the hospital. We can accept Uncle Larry's offer if you want."

"But *you* don't want to, do you?"

"Not really. I'd be pretty selfish to keep you here, though." He grinned crookedly, but his eyes were unsmiling.

"No. I don't really mind the hospital. It shouldn't be long till I'm on my feet, do you think?"

"I don't know. You won't be able to do anything with your right side for a while. I wouldn't want to leave you alone in the apartment all day. It seems Uncle Larry has offered the only solution. I'll swallow my pride and accept, I guess."

It was wrong. His reluctance ruined any elation I might have felt. His uncle, keen as he was, would sense Bruce's resentment and the cycle would resume.

"No, Bruce. We'll pray some more and not say anything until we feel better about it."

He kissed my forehead. "I'm sorry, Sandy. I shouldn't worry you now when you're just beginning to get well. I wish I were a better man. But I'm not."

"You're just fine for me. If you were perfect, you'd never want to be married to me."

"I can't imagine that — not being married to you. They laugh at people 'being made for each other,' but I think we were."

I brought up the subject which had haunted me for weeks.

"You've never asked — what was I doing in Adelbert Coogan's car?"

He shrugged. "It didn't worry me particularly, dear."

I shifted again, and received another reminder of that impulsive day.

"I hadn't seen him since he moved. Then — that day — it was so hot, and I missed the bus. He just happened to drive around the corner and offered me a ride. I expected him to drive me home, but he wanted to show off his new car. Then this other fellow challenged him to a drag race, and I couldn't make Del stop. That's all. He died without Christ. Isn't that awful?"

"It is. But he did hear. Lots of others never have."

"Was there a lot of curiosity? I mean, it didn't look very nice — a prospective missionary — a *pregnant* prospective missionary — in the car with a night club entertainer. Bruce, did you mind so much about the baby?"

"I minded more about you. You cried a lot after Dr. Mahoney told you the baby had died. I wished he'd not said anything."

"I think I asked him."

"Sandy, please — forget it. Everyone knows you're a warm, friendly girl. No one blames you for anything. We'll have other children, lots of them. But there never would be another Sandy for me."

"I must have been out of my head. I thought I'd killed her. Somehow when I was sick, it seemed my action had been deliberate."

His face became very bleak. "It was a bad time, Sandy. I

148

don't think it helps any to talk about it. Just remember — I love you. I always will. And if you still want to go to Uncle Larry's, it will be all right."

I shook my head. "No. I never want to do anything you don't want to do."

With a smile, he opened his textbook. The conversation had dredged up some very unpleasant memories, but at least we had been able to *talk*. It was progress.

Instead of Bruce appearing the following evening, Don and Pat both came in. This was most unusual, for whatever callers I had, always left the evening hours to Bruce.

"Bruce says he's sorry — he had an appointment tonight. Since I'm his brother, I'm elected to do the honors," Don explained in a grandiose attempt to be funny.

"What kind of appointment? He didn't mention one last night."

"He didn't say. In fact, he was pretty mysterious."

"Oh, Don, stop!" Pat protested. "You'll get her all curious, and probably it's only a dentist appointment."

"At night?" He changed the subject. "Hey, Sandy, I need an assistant in the shop. You want to work for me when you get out?"

I laughed. "That would be the end of a beautiful friendship. Why doesn't Pat help you?"

They exchanged glances of a secret warmly shared. "Pat's going to be busy in a few months."

They were so happily excited I could hardly wonder at their mystery. "Really? A baby? Are you sure?" I asked.

The very prospect lent Pat a radiance almost too beautiful to behold. "Dr. Mahoney says yes. Oh, Sandy, isn't it wonderful! The answer to all our prayers! It's just like that verse in the Bible, 'But seek ye first the kingdom of God and his righteousness, and all these things shall be added unto you.' "

In blind joy she gasped, "Sandy, thanks for not being jealous. Don and I were abominable about your baby — but you and Bruce — are — just — wonderful! Oh, do hurry and get well, so we can make plans together."

Every word was a turn of the screw. For just a moment I looked away, out the window at the street light which blinked intermittently with the shadow of leaves bounced against it in the cool October wind. Then I managed a smile.

"I'll try, Pat."

Something had happened to Bruce. I heard it in his step, no longer dragging, saw it in his face when he first pushed open the door.

"You want some news?" he asked needlessly. "I'm now a singer!"

"A singer?" I repeated, the word not making sense at first.

"A singer of songs, dear. I'm a member of the Dale Harrington Glee Club, with a TV program every Saturday night."

"What——? Dale Harrington! But he's *good,* Bruce!"

He grinned like a little boy. "So am I dear. Good enough to sing bass-baritone with his choral group. That's where I was last night, auditioning for Harrington himself."

"How did you ever know about it?"

"It was very odd. Of course, it was the Lord, but it looked like coincidence. I picked up a fare that night after I left you. He turned out to be Gene Desmond, the society reporter. You remember, he wrote up that little speech I made at the Club last spring. I didn't intend to speak to him, but he recognized me and remembered I could sing. He told me he'd heard about the vacancy with Harrington's group, took me into the studio to make an appointment, and that's where I went last night. He said he'd been wondering what happened to me – he was apparently quite impressed with our 'sincerity' as he describes it. Who would ever have thought——?"

His voice trailed back, as we both remembered back to Bruce's chagrin following his speech at the Club. I had been tremendously proud of him, but he had felt himself a fool.

"Cast thy bread upon the waters, for thou shalt find it after many days." We thought of the verse together.

"Bruce, isn't the Lord good? You can give up your taxi driving."

"Yes. I'll earn more with less time expended."

He sobered. I knew he had something more serious on his mind. "Sandy, I cut classes and went to see Uncle Larry this morning."

He paused. My heart fluttered in brief excitement. "What—?"

"I told him we'd be glad to accept his offer. Now that I can pay our way it doesn't seem so hard."

"Was it lack of money that bothered you?"

"Partly. I didn't want to be dependent on the old man again, but now – he seemed so pleased, though he tried to cover it up. You know how he is."

"Do you think it will matter with Don?"

150

"I went to his shop right after I talked with Uncle Larry. He was shocked at first; then he said he could forgive me for straightening out family matters if I could forgive him for being a father first."

"It's like a puzzle, isn't it? Or a play. All of a sudden, all the pieces begin to fit together. And we have a lovely picture. I wish I didn't get distressed about things. I wish I trusted the Lord completely."

"We're both learning. Maybe some day we'll be decent Christians."

He picked up my hand and kissed it.

The ambulance was black and shiny, but not particularly comfortable. My shoulder ached with fatigue.

We passed through the great iron gates, up the curving drive where elm trees, now denuded of all leaves, arched in stark beauty. The ambulance pulled to a halt at the side of the brownstone mansion. The driver and Bruce slid my stretcher out and carried it in through the sun porch door. There, in the family room, they were all gathered — Uncle Larry, Ellen, Tom. Eyes glistening with emotion, they settled me into the hospital bed set up before a large, cheerful bay window.

The outside door opened. The November wind swept into the room, causing everyone to turn in that direction. Hand in hand, Don and Pat stood shyly at the entrance, uncertain of their welcome.

Mr. King started with surprise. Mouths open, Tom and Ellen paused in their readjustment of the furniture. A frozen tableau, we hung a moment without movement. Then Uncle Larry crossed the room.

"Welcome home, kids," he said.